Glue

Dacia's Diary

D. W. PLATO

GLUE
DACIA'S DIARY

Author Credits: DW Plato, LLC
Cover art by John Phillip Cameron of Publishing Assist
Editing by Chelsea Pullano of Publishing Assist
Additional editing by Whitney Davis

iUniverse books may be ordered through booksellers or by contacting:

iUniverse
1663 Liberty Drive
Bloomington, IN 47403
www.iuniverse.com
1-800-Authors (1-800-288-4677)

ISBN: 978-1-5320-5388-7 (sc)
ISBN: 978-1-5320-5386-3 (hc)
ISBN: 978-1-5320-5387-0 (e)

Library of Congress Control Number: 2019900948

Print information available on the last page.

iUniverse rev. date: 04/30/2019

5 0772 08388047 9

To my daughter, with all my love—
without you, there would be no story

DACIA

1. The alcoholic virgin Roman goddess. She was a virgin because she was afraid to love again after her first love. She was famous for her sex appeal and her wonderful personality. She had a beautiful heart and body. She had a low self-esteem because her face wasn't usually as beautiful as her heart. Her heart was the purest and truest of the lands.
2. A word that infers something is cool, awesome, or hip.

—Urban Dictionary

CHAPTER 1

1993

If I were deranged, I could have walked into the bedroom, grabbed one of the dozen guns he collected, and shot him in the back of the head. All the odds were in my favor. At such close range, I would have hit him no matter how bad of a marksman I was. I'd planned every detail of my escape, but now that it was time, I almost couldn't go through with it. Instead of walking out the door, I found myself standing in our bedroom with the gun case open, wondering how difficult it would be to pull the trigger.

The gun felt heavy in my hand, but not cold. Weren't guns supposed to feel cold? It felt all wrong. I certainly liked a little naughtiness in my life, but not this kind of bad, not this kind of wrong.

An image of the bloody mess Leonard's head would make if it splattered on the wall appeared in my mind's eye. Chunks of his gray matter sliding down the wall onto the carpet finished the scene.

I thought of the double bloody mess if I shot first him and then myself. Would I put the gun in my mouth or hold it to my temple? Who would have to clean it up, or would they even bother? Our trailer would probably be condemned. Hauled away. I came to the conclusion our blood would commingle in some landfill forever. My stomach roiled. I put the gun back in the case and locked it. Breathing slowly, I reminded myself that everything was ready for my escape. My life was about to change.

Throughout our short-lived marriage, he had insisted on controlling everything, from what I wore to when I worked, when I went to bed, when I got up, and what I ate. He also took my money. He directly deposited my checks into a joint account from which he paid the bills. He would give me fifty dollars a week as an allowance, like I was his kid instead of his wife. God, I hated him. Little did he know that for the past year I'd hidden most of what I'd made. I'd created a tiny nest egg to start a new life and had slowly packed my belongings into four cardboard boxes, putting them into the back of a car. I did it little by little so he wouldn't notice. First my keepsakes, then my clothes. I didn't have much. Finally, the plan had come together … for the most part.

I left the cream-colored wedding dress hanging in the closet. Leonard had insisted that I wear that when we exchanged our vows in front of the justice of the peace. It was short and borderline slutty-looking, not really a wedding dress at all. He wouldn't let me wear heels and told me how I was to wear my hair. There had been no talk of whether I would change my last name; it was assumed I would. The biggest red flag I ignored was that he insisted on the traditional "obey" in my vows.

My stomach turned when I thought of how he'd stripped me of the last bit of my youth, as if his sole purpose had been to pluck me from my formative years and make me old, cynical, and cold. I was freaked out about uprooting my life, especially since it could create another "out of the frying pan into the fire" situation, but I knew I couldn't take one more day of this loveless, sexless marriage. I refused to be his doormat or pissing post any longer.

Although my husband wasn't physically abusive, he was verbally abusive, emotionally unavailable, and downright mean. His favorite pastime was to belittle me to others—friends, coworkers, or total strangers. Whoever would listen. His most common complaint was my cooking. He talked about me as if a woman's worth was found only in the kitchen.

"Bitch could burn water," he was known to mutter after describing something I had made. "Like burnt-mush goo," he would snicker. "Have you ever in your life had burnt-mush goo?"

I never learned to cook. My mom never taught me; her mom never taught her. The bedroom was the place to keep your man happy, or at least that's what she told me. As the old saying goes, I was young and dumb when I got married. My husband was only twenty months younger than my father—and twenty years older than me. Some people may have said I had daddy issues. Who was I to argue? As much as I hated to admit it, Leonard treated me more like a daughter than a wife. Perhaps *he* had daddy issues too.

As I continued thinking, the tacky wood-paneled walls seemed to be closing in on me. I looked down the hallway and stared at his mullet draping over the top of an overstuffed La-Z-Boy recliner, his hairy hand holding the remote control. My mind reeled back to when we met, how we ended up together. He; his wife, Jackie; and their dark-eyed daughter were my neighbors in the little trailer village that became my home when I took a job at Pipe Spring National Park in Arizona.

Their daughter, Christy, was a sweet little thing, polite and pretty. His wife was spicy in both her looks and her attitude.

One afternoon, Leonard showed up at my door with a fifth of Captain Morgan's rum and a few cans of Coke. I should have noticed the alcohol-to-soda ratio was way off. We drank, I smoked a little weed, and we drank some more. Once buzzed, we ended up on the couch. MTV's *Beavis and Butt-Head* played in the background for five minutes and then commercials for ten. During one ad break, he turned to me and kissed me. He jammed his hand hard between my legs and pulled them apart. "You're wet," he huffed.

"You're married," I replied. It was my only hesitation before our clothes came off.

Beavis was laughing that stupid guffaw of his as Leonard pushed inside me, grunting and groaning. All I remember thinking was *His back is hairy*. The rest was a rum-induced blur until he pulled out of me and grabbed me by my hair, trying to force his penis into my mouth. I clamped my lips shut as he came all over my face.

"I respect a woman that can take a good face shot." He laughed as he put his clothes back on. As he walked out my door, he took a slug from the quarter-full rum bottle. "Thanks, Dee," he said as he disappeared through the front door.

Later that night, someone came beating on my door, loud and angry like a cop knock, one that jolts you and leaves you startled out of your skin. I could see through the openings in the curtains that it was Leonard's wife. Quickly, I locked the door.

"You fucking tramp!" she screamed, still pounding on the door. I moved to the far side of the window to get a better view.

Leonard strode up behind her, saying, "I told you I was trading you in for a younger, sexier model."

"You bastard!" she screamed, and it was then that I noticed she was wielding a wooden baseball bat. "You made me abort my baby! You said we could fix things!" Mascara was streaming down her face, making it look masked and ugly.

My eyes flickered to their trailer, which was about twelve feet away from mine. I could see their daughter watching ringside like I was.

"You said you forgave me—that we could start over." Her rage was ebbing.

"Fix things?" he hissed. "Kind of hard to fix things when *it wasn't even my baby*! That's beyond fixable. You're a lying, cheating cunt! We're done."

"But you said you still loved me," she sobbed.

"I lied." Now his face contorted to ugliness too. "Payback's a bitch." He spat at her feet and stormed back to his front door. Their brown-eyed daughter's head disappeared from the window. I pictured her darting down the hallway to hide in her room. Leonard jerked the door open and then slammed it as the bat flew end over end, landing several feet short of him with a dull clatter.

"I hate you!" she bellowed toward their house. She turned toward my front door. "I hate you too!" Her fists pounded on the door, and I retreated to my room. Nervous energy caused me to lock that door too.

The next day, a U-Haul appeared, hooked to the back of her little Honda. Even though Leonard and I were married for eighteen months, I never saw her or their daughter again.

Chapter 2

I was smart enough to know that despite the fact Leonard had never been violent with me in the past, there's always a first time for shit like that. So the idea of confronting him made my knees shake and my palms sweat. Usually, he acted calm at first, and then—*Bam!* Insta-asshole.

Scanning the living room, I realized there wasn't anything in there I wanted. I honestly couldn't imagine missing this barren place or this barren relationship. It was now or never; I knew that much. Clearing my throat, I stood in front of him, deliberately blocking his view of the huge console television. "I'm leaving you," I said and braced myself for the blowback.

"Do what ya gotta do," he said and craned his neck to see the screen. He touched the buttons on the remote control, surfing the five hundred channels of garbage. For a moment, I thought he hadn't heard me or he didn't understand what I was saying.

"Um, okay," I squeaked out. "Goodbye?" It came out as more of a question than a statement, and I felt foolish.

"Good luck, Dacia." His tone was flat, no hint of emotion.

What? Is this really happening? Just like that? My facial muscles relaxed.

For a moment, I thought he agreed with me and our split would be amicable, but then he added the punch. "You'll need all the luck you can get because you don't have any goddamn skills." He looked up to the ceiling, reconsidering. "Well, hoeing, maybe, but you ain't even that good at fuckin'. Ain't no one gonna want you. You're worthless." He took a long slug of his Coors Light and belched, loud and wet. "Fucking worthless."

My stomach clenched into a knot. *Worthless.* A wave of panic crested over my whole being as his eyes met mine and he shook his head. *Could he be right? Am*

I ruined? Again, I hated feeling like I was his kid. What was I doing? I glanced behind me at the car loaded with my things. Doubt poured over me. He had ruined me.

Perhaps he could change into the man I thought I'd married. *Maybe I should wait it out,* I thought. Was my life really *that* bad? Maybe it *was* me. *Perhaps I should try to be a better wife.* If I was ruined and worthless, what would I have to do to fix myself?

An uncomfortable silence hung between us as I waited for him to say more. I looked around at the trailer I had called home for over two years. A heaviness settled over me, suffocating me. *Should I stay or go?* When I thought of staying, I felt nothing. No sadness, no happiness, nothing. When I thought of leaving, tears stung my eyes. A knot tied in my throat. Feeling sad was better than not feeling at all.

"Do you still love me?" I managed to ask.

"This union was never about love." His eyes narrowed, and his attention shifted back to the television. I silently counted to ten and then turned and walked out, my hands shaking, my knees weak.

As I left, I didn't slam the door, although I wanted to slam it hard enough to make our wedding picture crash to the floor and shatter into a million pieces. I wanted to scream at him—to take Jackie's bat and smash the television. In my mind, I pictured myself swinging it at his head as he sat rooted to the recliner, remote in hand.

My heart raced in my chest and my stomach clenched into knots as I headed for the car. He must not have thought I was being serious. This was no bluff; I had to leave or face his scorn for threatening him.

As I shifted the car into reverse, he appeared on the porch. He must have looked in my nightstand and seen that the few important items in my life were no longer there. For a moment, I thought he'd profess his love. Ask—no, beg—me to stay. For one fleeting second, I pictured myself bounding back into his arms and our marriage turning into something wonderful. Hope rose in my chest. The corners of my lips trembled, and I waited for—

"You stupid, fucking bitch!" he screamed, interrupting my imagination. "You worthless cunt! You're nothing without me! Nothing! Leave! Go be worthless on your own time. You're a nobody!"

His tirade continued. He threw his half-empty beer at my windshield, hitting the glass with a tinny clatter. As the can rolled off the hood and into the overgrown weeds, I backed out.

Nervous bile boiled in my gut. My mind played his words again. *Good luck, Dacia. You're going to need it.* The way he'd said my name, laced with venom, made me ill. *Worthless.* His hiss repeated over and over in my anxiety-driven mind. *This union was never about love.* Tears tumbled down my cheeks as I wished for a fairy godmother to appear, wave her magic wand, and make my bad choices of men disappear.

As I got on the freeway and headed north, my mind wandered back through my relationship with Leonard, the roller-coaster ride. When it was good, it was good, but when it was bad, it was horrible! I drove by a billboard advertising a local restaurant. A huge steak was featured, cut open to display the inside, cooked to a perfect medium rare. A memory of grilling steaks popped into my head, Leonard and me drinking a beer and watching the early-evening clouds roll toward us. About the time it started raining, the propane ran out on the grill. I took the meat inside and turned on the broiler to finish cooking them. I heard the truck pull out of the driveway and looked out to see Leonard drive off as the rain began to pelt the ground.

Thirty or so minutes later, I had the steaks in the oven, broiling. I was watching them through the lit window of the oven door. Leonard walked in, drenched.

"Where's the beef?" he asked. I giggled, remembering a commercial for a fast-food chain from when I was a kid.

"Right here," I replied as I grabbed the hot pad and pulled out the plate and set it gently on the stove top. When I looked at Leonard, I could tell something was wrong. A shadow had slipped over his handsome features.

"I don't eat broiled meat," he sneered.

"Don't be ridiculous; of course you do. Restaurants broil their steaks to get the temperature—" Before I could finish my sentence, he grabbed the plate and threw it across the room.

"I don't eat broiled meat!" he screamed. "Fuck you—I burned my fingers. I hope you're happy." He turned and walked down the hall to our bedroom, mumbling, "Thanks for nothing, you worthless bitch."

Other recollections pinged in my head, accompanied by the heavy emotions tied to the memories. A sign announced I was a little over two hundred miles from my hometown. Just seeing the words brought up memories of my mother. I glanced in the rearview mirror, and her eyes stared back. They were the color of my dad's but the shape of hers.

Another memory played in my mind's eye, one that started out sweet. A random thought—my parents together, happy. My mom was smiling at my dad, love filling her eyes. Damien couldn't have been older than first- or second-grade age, making me two or three years old. Was that the last—no, the *only*—time I ever saw her look at my dad in that way? I scanned my childhood, my adolescence; I couldn't recall. She was usually cross with him. In fact, during the last conversation I had with her, she was furious at him over how much he drank or how little money he made. She seemed to always be stressed when it came to him—to them.

And she never complained to him directly, only to my brother and me. It was one of those things, those questions that haunted me: Did he cause her blood to boil? Did the pressure to rise enough to make up for his flaws and cause the hemorrhage that was her demise? It was something I couldn't dwell on, or else it made me sick.

Another memory—me on the phone to her, telling her I had got married. Her one syllable reply: "Why?" Weirdly enough, that thought made me smile.

Despite my dysfunctional parents, I graduated with honors from high school a year ahead of schedule in Central Utah, otherwise known as "Mormon country." In that neck of the woods, if students didn't bother taking seminary classes, they could get ahead each semester, and I played that to my advantage. Since my family wasn't Mormon, I was way ahead in school by the time I turned eighteen. I thrived on the debate team, playing to my chatty strengths. If there was one thing I was best at, it was talking.

When I got my diploma, and exited the public school scene, I thought I was on top of the world. I had dated a few guys, but only the overly hormonal ones who wanted to date me just to get laid. I don't mean that in an arrogant "damn, I'm hot" kind of way; it was just a fact, an "I like sex, and it shows" kind of thing. What was wrong with a woman enjoying sex as much as guys did? Nothing, as far as I could tell.

After a few years of college, I met Leonard. The relationship was so strange, because before we got married, he seemed to adore me; he showered me with expensive dinners, jewelry, lingerie, and clothes and sent me flowers on our one-month anniversary. He left love notes on the windshield of my car when I was at work and even swept me off to Vegas and Los Angeles for weekend getaways. But once I agreed to marry him, everything changed. I became his midlife crisis. Everything that was wrong with the world was my fault. They wore on me, his insults and cut-downs.

Eventually, I drove right past where I had grown up, but I had no desire to stop. Naturally, my thoughts tumbled back to my childhood, more reminiscing about my parents. The cemetery where my mom's tombstone stood crossed my mind, but it wasn't a place I wanted to visit on a whim. I do miss her. Every day, I miss her. One day, she was there, my best friend, my closest confidante, and then she was gone the next, stolen from me by a random brain aneurysm—devastating, to say the least. It was she who named me. I thought about that sometimes, being the original weird-name kid. To this day, I've never met another Dacia.

It's pronounced "Day-sha," if you were wondering. "De-ja," like déjà vu, is the California version. "Da-cee-a" (which rhymes with Garcia) is the New Mexican or Spanish version. "Darci" is the "oh, I didn't really pay attention to the spelling" pronunciation. My parents were hippies in the '60s, so I guess I should be glad my name isn't Rainbow Dancer or some shit like that, but it's still never easy for anyone to pronounce.

Then came a flashback of elementary school, how I was teased. "Douche-a," the boys would cry and mock me. "Pizza Face" and "Crater Face" were also popular taunts. "Medusa" was another name that both the boys and the girls called me. As an adult, I've wondered if it was really a hard-core slam. Medusa, after all, caught the eye of Poseidon; she was the most beautiful daughter. Her snake hair and the whole "one look turns you to stone" curse came from a jealous rival. As a kid, though, that shit hurt. I hated school. The other students were mean. Nowadays, it's called *bullying*; then, it was just *kids being kids*.

My dad and I had never been close, but when he remarried after my mom died, our relationship became nonexistent. I have one older brother, Damien, who lives in Albuquerque, New Mexico, with his wife, but they aren't around much—even during the holidays, when they stay with her family. It seemed he fled south into the arms of her family only minutes after burying our mother. I miss him. When I moved to Arizona, I hoped we would be closer, but it didn't happen.

I try to be happy for my brother; I do. I'm glad he has his dark-haired family that rallies around everything he does. I am happy that he has his wife and her tight-knit circle of relatives. Otherwise, he'd be as lonely as I am.

Within a matter of days, I'd report to my new job at a call center in Northern Utah, five hundred miles from where I lived with Leonard. When I'd given my two weeks' notice to my supervisor, I'd made it clear that my departure needed to stay confidential. Thankfully, she had been cool about it. She knew the story of Jackie's infidelity. Nobody blamed me for her and Leonard's divorce. Everyone knew how Leonard and I had become a couple. Only about a hundred people lived in our tiny trailer village. Everyone's business was just that: everyone's business.

For my new housing, I had found a room with a woman—a single mama with a boy and a girl—who desperately needed the cash a temporary roommate would bring. Although I hadn't seen the house, I had agreed, as it had five bedrooms! I'd have my own room and bathroom and would share the common spaces and everything else. The price was right, and she didn't want a huge deposit. It was doable, unlike the situation with my husband.

When I arrived at my new home, it looked exactly as I had imagined it would, a yellow-and-white Victorian-style house with dainty flower gardens lining both sides of the large porch. Suzy, my new landlady/roommate, appeared in the doorway. She greeted me with her sweet, friendly brown eyes and a bright smile. "Hello. You must be Dacia." Her skin had the color and texture of that of a woman who fake-tans too much, but it didn't matter, because her fit body and perky chest made up for it. Not to mention she was hot! I nodded and moved up the walkway.

"Nice to meet you," I said, extending my hand for her to shake. Inside, Suzy showed me my living area, which was a large upper-floor room with a walk-in closet and a small bathroom containing a shower, a sink, and a toilet—the basics. It was great at just $250 a month. As Suzy showed me around the house, her kids—Erick, age ten, and Ellie, age eight—ran multiple circles around us, their bright, intelligent eyes checking me out as they smiled at me mischievously.

As I introduced myself, I could tell they were sizing me up. As the youngest in my family, I'd done my fair share of being a little monster, and my immediate plan with Suzy's children was to outbrat the brats. I wondered if I was overreacting to their rambunctiousness, but Suzy pretty much confirmed my suspicions when she indicated that the last roommate had made a hasty exit because of a conflict with the children. I considered the better plan might be to avoid them altogether. Avoid, avoid, avoid.

During the first weekend at my new place, I found I was still living out of my suitcase. The dresser remained empty, although my four cardboard boxes sat atop it, still taped shut. I wandered around my new neighborhood, trying to heal my heart. I didn't miss Leonard, per se, but I did miss the daily routine. I missed being someone's wife. Besides Suzy, I didn't have any friends here. I couldn't really call her a friend either. I mean, we lived together, but we didn't really have any type of connection or any conversations.

One afternoon, I wandered into the local 7-Eleven. I suddenly reminisced about my youth, and a craving for nachos with jalapeños, my favorite fattening snack as a teenager, pushed me through the glass doors, the familiar ding deepening the memories.

"Welcome to 7-Eleven," the cashier said as she rang up a pack of cigarettes for a customer. Confusion and shock overwhelmed me. Was I still experiencing a flashback? My best friend from childhood was the cashier. I blinked like a deer caught in the proverbial headlights. It was like thinking about my past made it appear, materialize in front of my eyes.

I'd only seen Kristine twice since high school—once at her wedding the year after we graduated and once at my mom's funeral two years later. I thought she lived in Nevada, not Utah. But there she stood, wearing a red uniform shirt and too-tight jeans, her face caked in makeup, and, as usual, laughing too loud. She greeted folks with a bright smile as they entered. She hadn't changed a bit—still cute and bubbly, thin with great tits. Her big hair and long fake nails changed colors depending on the season. Currently, she was blonde and had bright blue nail tips. I stood, gaping at her, rooted to the nostalgia.

Once recognition sunk in, she ran around the counter, squealing like a middle-school girl, and flung her arms around me. But seriously, what were the odds that she worked in my new neighborhood and that I happened to walk in during her part-time shift? Fate can be cruel.

With a smattering of words, she filled me in on her life as she rang up Big Gulps and gas purchases. "Still married," she informed me and told me about her daughter, who I remembered from a Christmas card. I made a large nachos with extra peppers and munched on them as we chatted. They didn't taste quite like I remembered, something about the chips, or maybe it was the cheese. They were a bit disappointing.

"So, Dacia, still a four-twenty kinda gal?" Kris asked, giving me a wink.

"Well, duh." My luck improved further. I had run into not only an old friend but one I knew could score me some bud in the first week I'd reconnected with her. "Mary Jane" had always been good to me. I had smoked pot nearly my whole life, until Leonard. Once we were married, he suddenly decided he couldn't have it in the house or be around someone smoking all the time. *Hello?* I wanted to tell him. *I smoked before. I smoked weed in the short time we dated!* And it was *my* house! I quit for him because it wasn't worth the fight.

"Stoners are stupid," he would say. "I didn't marry a dummy."

But now? Leonard was far behind me, and the idea of a nice doobie sounded euphoric. Bumping into Kristine was perfect. Finally, the universe had aligned for me, and just in time. I had found a great place to live, had bumped into my old friend with weed, and had the promise of a fresh job. A fresh start to life was exactly what I needed.

My new job was nothing more than a typical call-center job, but it had the added benefit of free standby flights on the airline I was now booking reservations on. The job wasn't hard—tedious and monotonous, yes, but not hard. Once we sold a seat on a flight, we would go to the dry-erase board where each flight was written. We would indicate the sale with a hash mark on the date, handwrite the ticket, and give it to the supervisor, who ensured it was mailed to the proper address and had an extra pamphlet added with our fare rules and baggage-allowance details.

During training, I was paired up with two women to do some role-playing: Joy, a sixty-something hippie with light pink hair who was a licensed massage therapist and got the job at the airline specifically for the flight benefits; and Mari, a blonde-haired, green-eyed dreamer. The faraway look in her eyes always made me wonder where she was. She had the most annoying habit of twisting her hair around her little finger; the tip would turn a weird red-purple color, and she'd tug it free.

We made learning the three-letter airport codes into a game. "SMF, silly motherfucker," Mari said. "You know, like it's silly Sacramento is the capital of California and not LAX or SFO."

"Big Nashville Airport, BNA," Joy said with a smile.

I began to sing, "CMH, pure cane sugar, from Ohio, born in the sun."

"It's C and H, pure cane sugar, from Hawaii," Joy corrected me.

Mari and I looked at each other and began to sing in harmony, "CMH, pure cane sugar, from Ohio …" Laughter bubbled out of our mouths as we finished.

Joy shook her head and tried to hide a little smile. "CMH, Columbus, Ohio; that's one I won't soon forget."

The three of us stuck together through the entire training. The more I got to know them, the more I liked them both, genuinely. Mari was pretty, quiet, and observant. Her green eyes sparkled and danced when she spoke but became serious when she listened. And Joy, with her pink wispy hair adorned with a feather clip, was likable, although definitely weird. And when I say *weird*, I mean *weird*, like claiming she heard angels talking to her, not to mention the fact that she said she could see the auras and energies of people. She told me her hands were blessed by the heavens and she could heal with her massages and channel Divine Light into the people she touched. Who was I to question her? Maybe she could do all of that.

It hadn't been but a few weeks, and I'd already shed the skin of my old life. I was young and vibrant but felt I had missed out on my youth. The divorce was swift, and my new Utah driver's license reverted my name back to my Danish maiden name of Pederson. Because of my family's background, I had always liked to picture a Viking heritage for myself; it matched my stature and coloring, and okay—who was I kidding?—my attitude as well.

When I received my first paycheck, I splurged and went to a wine festival in Park City. The majestic mountains in their late spring glory, the flowers in full bloom, and the sky of perfect blue, which even Crayola would have a hard time duplicating, were beyond gorgeous. And when I combined that with the music, food, and wine, the experience made me feel literally light with giddiness. I hadn't been this happy in years. If only I had someone to share it with. Yes, I felt happy, but lonely too.

As I strolled along the streets lined with vendors, I noticed one tent selling crystals wrapped in artistic wire. A particular piece, an amethyst laced with silver and hanging from a black leather cord, drew me in like a magnet. I picked it up and carefully studied the stone. Shaped like a sloppily drawn teardrop, it had the darkest purple coloring I had ever seen; yet it grew lighter toward the narrower end. I picked it up half a dozen times before I finally bought it.

When I put it around my neck, its heaviness reminded me of the ball and chain I had left and the freedom I had found. It was a sign. It was time for a new chapter. Oh hell, it was time for a new book altogether.

CHAPTER 3

The first six months of living with Suzy and her kids flew by. My only problem was my overactive imagination. For some reason, I felt stressed Leonard would show up on my doorstep. If I heard a news clip about a murder, I wondered if he was going to come for me. I thought of all the guns he owned, what a great shot he was, his temper.

A couple of times, I got completely freaked out about it. I worked myself up into an unavoidable frenzy. For example, when a car I didn't recognize parked in front of our house or a call from someone who hung up on my answering machine came from a number I didn't recognize, I thought for sure it was him. Talk about paranoia.

In time, I came to realize I just wasn't that important to him. My life improved every day. I formed a stable relationship with Suzy—we were nice to each other but not super close. Work went well enough, and on my off days, I made a habit of flying to Vegas, enjoying the anonymity of being whoever I wanted to be.

Additionally, Kristine and I picked up right where we had left off in high school, with her becoming my close friend and pot dealer overnight. We reminisced about dancing to the *Grease* soundtrack in fourth grade and crushing on Tim LeBron in eighth. Since Kristine was prettier than me, I comfortably slid into the background whenever we went out. With her, I liked being the chatty sidekick. I could talk about anything to anyone. One of my favorite black light posters from my childhood read, "If you can't dazzle them with brilliance, baffle them with bullshit." It could have almost been my motto.

Summer slipped into fall. Although my birthday doesn't fall on Halloween, I have always celebrated the two events together. Excited for me to begin my twenty-fourth year as a single woman, Kristine suggested we celebrate at City

Limits, the local club that had become our regular hangout spot. City Limits was a long and skinny rectangular building. Pool tables and bathrooms were on one end, a small stage and dance floor on the other. A few booths lined the wall across from the bar, and several tables were peppered in between. With local bands and no cover charge, it was a convenient, cheap place to celebrate. I ended up inviting Suzy, and she offered to be the designated driver for the evening.

Kristine and Dave, her tall, dark, and handsome husband, met us there. When I met her man, I was instantly drawn to his good looks, but after a moment or two of forcing a conversation with him, I realized his beauty was the only thing he had going for him.

As the evening progressed, Joy stopped by and brought me a present—a bright yellow scarf, my least favorite color. As she wrapped the scarf around my neck, she noticed the necklace I'd bought for myself at the wine festival. "Whoa, that stone's energy is one to be harnessed." Hovering her hand over it, she closed her eyes and hummed softly. I glanced at Suzy, who was stifling a smirk as she watched us.

Joy took several deep breaths and said, "Thank you," to the air above her head and turned to me. "You should stop by my cubicle sometime; we can release some of that negativity you're carrying around. My hands are magic, remember?"

"I'm not carrying around negativity," I blurted. I toasted her with my drink. "This is the happiest I've been in my entire life." She gave me a quizzical look. "For real!" I insisted.

Just then, Mari sauntered in with a bunch of helium-filled balloons and a bag that looked suspiciously like it contained alcohol. "Happy birthday, beautiful!" she said as she threw her arms around me, the balloons dancing overhead. She whispered in my ear, "Brought you the good stuff for the after-party."

I noticed that although Joy smiled at Mari, Joy's body tensed as her eyes filled with sadness. She finished her drink and bade the group farewell. As she hugged me, she whispered in my ear, "If you lie with dogs—"

"What?" I abruptly pulled away from her.

Simply, she responded, "Happy birthday, Dacia," and put her hand under my chin like I was a child. Our eyes met. "Be safe, dear one."

"Um … okay," I muttered as she walked away.

"Did you get a new mama for your birthday?" Mari joked as I returned to the table. I shot her a dirty look.

Christopher and Cory were two dudes I had seen at the bar multiple times. I could count on one of them being there any night of the week. Christopher, short with dark hair, and Cory, tall and blond, had noticed the crowd at our table. They sauntered over and ordered a round of shots for everyone.

As we scooted the chairs around to make room for them, Kristine whispered,

"Brought you a little birthday treat." She winked and motioned toward the bathroom. "Like the good ole days."

Mari smiled. "That sounds like something I want to get in on."

And with that, the three of us excused ourselves to the ladies' room, where we crammed into the handicap stall. Kris took from her purse a folded square of paper that had been cut from a magazine and folded into a tiny envelope approximately an inch by an inch and a half. Next, she pulled out a CD, *Achtung Baby* by U2. Carefully, she opened the bindle and poured out a small pile of cocaine. With her driver's license, she chopped and shaped three little white lines.

"Wow, I haven't done blow in ages," Mari whispered excitedly.

"Me neither," I said as I rolled a dollar bill into a straw. As I inhaled, my heart rate picked up speed, and my eyes felt as if they wanted to explode out of my eye sockets. Kris traded me items and did her line as Mari moved her hair to one side and snorted hers in turn.

"Thanks, friend," I said to Kris as I rubbed my finger over the remains on the CD case and then over my gums.

"Yeah, thanks," Mari added warmly as we exited the stall together.

"Oh, by the way," Kris said as she looked at me, "Dave's mad at me because I told him I was sharing with you instead of him, selfish little prick." She rolled her eyes. "He's fine as long as he doesn't have to share me with anyone, but as soon as my attention is diverted, he turns into a little bitch."

"Leonard was like that," I mumbled.

"It's why I stay single," Mari interjected, even though Kris was obviously talking to me. Kris gave me a look as if to say, *Who is this woman?* I put my arm around my old friend as we walked back to join the others.

Upon our return, I immediately noticed a handsome man I'd never seen before sitting in my seat talking to Suzy. Her face brightened when she saw us approach.

"Here's the birthday girl!" she said with way too much excitement. The man glanced up at me and moved over so I could sit down, offering me birthday well-wishes.

"I'm Jack," he introduced himself, extending his hand. "Sorry to crash your party, but I was drawn to all you pretty ladies like a magnet to steel! You don't mind if I join your party?"

Despite Suzy vehemently shaking her head no, no, no, I agreed. I was curious to watch how Jack, who was obviously enamored with Suzy, would proceed. I inwardly giggled as he slid his chair over, leaned in, and whispered into her ear.

"I'm taken," she exclaimed loudly and turned to me, her eyes begging me to go along with whatever excuse she made up. "Ready? I really need to get the babysitter home by midnight."

"We should get going too." Kristine stood, grabbing her jacket from the back of a chair. Dave bolted up, ready to dash out the door as soon as Kris said the word.

"Thanks for coming! I think I'm gonna stay a little bit longer," I said as I stood and gave my friends affectionate hugs.

"Sure you'll be all right?" I could see the worry in Suzy's eyes. With my most sincere smile, I assured her I would be just fine.

Dave raised his hand in a half-assed goodbye wave. "Happy birthday," he mumbled as they all walked away.

After everyone left, Jack ordered the next round for Cory, Christopher, Mari, and me. Seconds later, Mari motioned toward the restroom, and we left the three men deep in conversation.

"Got any more treats?" Mari asked as soon as we were alone. Kris *had* given me the folded bindle. It made me wonder if Mari had noticed or if she'd made a lucky guess. I nodded, and we used the end of a pen cap for a bump—a little snort of the blow.

"You gonna be okay if I bail?" she asked.

"You're leaving?"

"Yeah, in a minute."

I sniffed another small pile of the white powder. "Yeah, I'll be fine. If I don't take Jack home and jump his bones, I'll get Christopher to run me back to Suzy's."

"Okay. Have fun with that." She grinned.

We rejoined the gentlemen just as Christopher and Cory said their goodbyes. I watched as Mari slipped Cory her phone number written in a matchbook. When Christopher hugged me goodbye, he looked into my eyes and wished me happy birthday. The passion in his well-wishes caught me off guard until I realized how much he was slurring his words. He was definitely drunk.

When it was down to Jack and me, we moved to the bar top and ordered more drinks. I slipped into the bathroom one more time for a little more coke, and when I returned, Jack looked me up and down in a way he hadn't before.

"What?" I giggled.

"I guess you'll have to do tonight."

"What do you mean?" My eyes narrowed, my lips growing pencil thin in frustration at what I knew was coming.

"Well, I was hoping to fuck your roommate, but you'll have to do."

"Fuck you." I took a long drink of my cocktail to avoid his gaze.

"Oh, don't be butt-hurt." He smiled, and I noticed how much better he looked when he showed some teeth. "It'll still be fun," he insisted, his voice playful and kind. "Besides, it's your birthday." I cocked one eyebrow and met his eyes. "You want to get laid on your birthday, don't you?" he continued.

I took another sip of my drink, contemplating how to answer. "What the fuck." I sighed. "Sure."

He leaned in and kissed me, his tongue pushing into my mouth with aggression. I wasn't sure if it was meant to be a turn-on or his idea of foreplay, or if it was just a drunken maneuver that seemed appropriate but wasn't.

After arriving at his apartment, Jack helped me finish my cocaine and busted out a birthday bindle of his own. We stayed up most of the night. We had sex in his room, in the kitchen, in the backyard, and on the roof of his house—yeah, the roof. We climbed out of his bedroom window to smoke a little weed and ended up doing it up there too. It was a fun fuck fest, which certainly makes me sound slutty, but hell, it *was* my birthday.

We finished the last of the drugs in the living room. As we finished, he laughed and told me he thought his dick was rubbed raw from all the fucking we'd done. I laughed and called him a pussy. Jack winked at me and told me he had a charged dildo if I hadn't had enough.

A few hours later, the smell of coffee woke me. As I rubbed my eyes, I noticed a rumpled pillow on the floor next to the couch and assumed Jack had slept there. I heard him talking to someone in the other room but couldn't make out what he was saying.

Trying to gauge the time, I poked my head over the back of the couch to peer into the kitchen. Jack, wrapped in a blanket draped like a toga over his torso, stood in the kitchen, talking to a shirtless man in tight white jeans, his chiseled chest tanning-bed brown. My breath caught in my throat. Who the hell was this? His blue eyes sparkled, and his blond hair, just out of the shower, fell in tight ringlets around his head. He laughed at something Jack said. He had a great smile, and I couldn't help but grin myself. Jack saw me, picked up a small tray, and walked back to the living room.

"Good morning," he greeted me as he set down the tray. I reached for a steaming mug of coffee. "Don't mind my half-dressed roommate; he's harmless." Setting the coffee back down, I reached for a spoon and one of the two grapefruit halves on the tray and glanced behind me. Shirtless white-pants dude sat at the kitchen table reading the back of a cereal box as he ate.

"Last night was fun." Jack smiled, scooping out a section of grapefruit. I nodded and dug into my citrus, my eyes involuntarily darting back to the kitchen.

"Yeah," I agreed. *Fun for my birthday*, I thought, *but it will never go any further.* I wasn't even that attracted to Jack. Damn, where in the world was his roommate last night?

"Gotta ask you something important, though," Jack said. Feeling confused, I looked at him as he continued. "You gonna be mad at me if I fuck your roommate?"

I set down the grapefruit and took a sip of the coffee, taking a deep breath, inhaling the rich aroma, savoring the moment. This was not the question I had expected. Before answering, I paused as if deep in thought. I glanced again at the blond-haired, blue-eyed shirtless guy at the kitchen table and shook my head. "Would you be mad if I fucked yours?"

CHAPTER 4

My life was so mundane—the call center's gray walls, the cubicle where I spent eight to ten hours a day, the script I said over and over. I felt confident the windowless break room was painted a pale yellow just to brighten the place. Was it better or worse than where I started? I reminded myself it was better to feel sad than to not feel at all.

On workdays, I had taken up rollerblading in Liberty Park, which was just a few blocks from my house. I'd smile at the young mothers pushing their strollers and the elderly couples strolling hand in hand.

On weekends, the park would be packed. I loved listening to the drum circles or talking to the stoned hippies about the way life used to be. It always made me smile when I saw kids with lemonade stands; I'd usually buy two glasses. I felt as if I was on the fringe of belonging here.

The work schedules were decided based on bids and seniority. Since I hadn't worked at the call center long, I usually had Tuesday and Wednesdays off, which was fine; I made a habit of flying to Vegas early on Tuesdays, when flights were relatively open. Traveling standby was nothing more than glorified hitchhiking, so I got used to traveling when no one else wanted to. Since my shift didn't start until three in the afternoon, I would stay in Vegas until Thursday morning and fly home in time for my shift. Of course, I went alone and fantasized about having friends, or a lover, who would travel with me. I craved an intimate relationship, longed for someone to make me whole.

Salt Lake International was white and shiny, so much so it reminded me of a hospital, sterile and monotone, a bit like the people who worked there. One week, the airport wasn't very crowded, so I felt fairly confident I'd get on the flight.

Since I had to wait for all paying passengers to board before I could, I lounged against a wall and listened for the customer service agent to call my name.

"Fancy meeting you here."

I looked around to see who had spoken to me. Mari struck a pose similar to mine, leaning against the wall three feet away. I smiled and waved and turned my attention back to the customer service agent's announcements.

Mari wasn't ready to give up. "Really? Vegas? Boring!" I raised my eyebrows as I turned to look at her. She continued as she studied her ticket. "You should change your destination."

"Oh really? To where?" I challenged her.

"San Jose," she suggested, as if it were obvious and I was an idiot for not knowing.

"So, I'm assuming that's where you're headed?" I asked.

"Yep! You should come. Great nightlife." She winked.

"Better than Sin City?" I chuckled as my name came over the loudspeaker for standby clearance. With a bit of surprise, I heard myself ask the customer service agent, "How hard would it be to change my ticket to San Jose?"

"Not hard at all." With a smile, she reissued my ticket and handed me a purple plastic card with large numbers reading 101. I ambled back to Mari and took my place against the wall.

She noticed the color of my card matched hers. "So, you're comin'?" I nodded. She looked at her shoes and smiled as the boarding announcement for the San Jose flight came over the PA.

Mari had a car parked in long-term parking in San Jose. In the back seat, I noticed half a male mannequin, which she proceeded to wrestle out of the two-door coupe. Holding the mannequin awkwardly, she popped the trunk.

"You're in the back, Freddie," she grunted, shoving it into the trunk of the car.

"Freddie?"

"Yeah, I put him in the passenger side so I can drive in the carpool lane." She threw her bag in the back seat and got in.

"So, let me get this straight. You invited me to San Jose so you can drive in the HOV lane with a clear conscience?" I joked.

"Yeah, exactly," she said, deadpan serious.

After she paid the attendant for parking, I did the math in my head. The car had been here five days. She pulled away from the airport and headed to the closest convenience store. Handing me a fifty, she instructed me to pay for forty dollars of gas and to get two cups of ice, two Sprites, and a large pack of gum.

"What flavor gum?" I asked. She shrugged.

When I returned with the goods, she had finished filling up the car. "Doublemint, my favorite," she commented.

"My mom's too." I smiled.

She extracted a CD case from the glove box: Tears for Fears. I nodded in approval as I watched her rummage through the console and then pull out a small silver case. With the ease of a professional, she dumped the contents of the container onto the flat surface of the CD case and drew up two even lines. Seemingly from nowhere, she produced a straw that had been cut to a couple of inches long and snorted one of the lines.

"Looks like I picked the wrong week to quit sniffing glue," Mari said, handing me the CD.

"Hm, I thought you said the other night you hadn't done coke in eons?" I stated, snorting the other line.

"It's not coke; it's crystal."

"Crystal?" I squeaked as my nose began to burn and my eyes watered. Bile bubbled from my gut as the car seemed to tilt several degrees. I tried to focus on Mari, but her voice sounded like it had traveled down a long tube.

"Aw shit. You've never done meth?" she asked me. With trembling hands, I flung the door open just in time to empty my stomach, followed by a few rounds of dry heaves. "Sorry, girl," Mari said sympathetically when I returned to my seat. My hands shook as I accepted a Sprite from her. I took a long swig before realizing it had Captain Morgan's spiced rum in it.

"Dude, it's not even ten o'clock," I said, choking a little, eyes still runny. My stomach wasn't sure if it was grateful for the Sprite or pissed I had just downed a shot of rum. It gurgled, and I thought I might be sick again. I sat back in the passenger seat and took deep breaths as the drugs coursed through my veins. It felt as if my brain was bleeding.

"It's almost 1:00 p.m. in New York," she stated, sipping her own drink as she maneuvered into the freeway's carpool lane, heading south. I kept my window down and enjoyed the fresh air as the cityscape gave way to rural farmland, crowded with immigrants wearing big straw hats harvesting the fields.

Thankfully, the Sprite settled my stomach, but I was completely wired, higher than I had ever been in my life. Blood surged through my veins, my eyelids opened wider than usual, and my jaw began to work its way back and forth, grinding my teeth. It felt as if we were speeding, going a hundred miles an hour. I glanced at the speedometer, sixty-five on the nose.

Eventually, Mari took the Salinas exit and drove onto a dirt road that led to one of the farms. She stopped at two large, windowless metal buildings. They were identical in size and shape with large bay doors on the front and a smaller, person-sized door on the side. An older brick silo could be seen farther off. A group of men picking vegetables caught my eye. I jumped when Mari tapped her horn. She flashed the high beams and then downed the rest of her cocktail in one gulp. As she got out, she popped a piece of the gum into her mouth.

One of the men glanced up and said something to another worker, who looked up; a broad smile overtook his sun-worn face. A flicker of light reflected off what appeared to be a gold tooth. His shirt was stained with sweat, and his jeans were loose, caked at the leg hems with dried dirt. With excitement exuding from every pore, he started toward the car.

"Be right back," Mari told me. She got out and motioned with her head toward the two buildings. She and the man disappeared through the small door and five minutes later reappeared. She walked with purpose to the car, her face beet red. A few seconds later, the man appeared and ambled over to one of the trucks parked in the shade. He lit a cigarette and watched Mari as she backed out of the driveway. She loudly popped the gum as she waved and gave him one of the fakest smiles I'd ever seen.

"God, I hate that man," she said through gritted teeth. "Bartender!" she demanded, handing me her glass of ice. I mixed her another drink and handed it back. "I guess I picked the wrong week to quit drinking." And with one breath, she chugged half of it.

Once we were back on the freeway, she reached into her bra and pulled out a cut corner of a large baggie that had been tied into a knot. Yellow powder expanded the plastic into a triangular ball. She tossed it into the center console and spat her gum out the window.

"Roll us up a jay," she said and opened the ashtray to reveal a pack of rolling papers and several marijuana buds.

I couldn't feel my brain; it seemed disconnected from my body. "I might be sick again," I managed to mumble.

"Well then, the pot will settle your stomach," she stated with a sly grin.

CHAPTER 5

The next exit was Monterey. A few turns brought us into a well-groomed neighborhood. The houses were spaced far apart, and fields lined the backyards. Several houses had corrals and horses, others huge gardens or overgrown swaths of land. It was exactly what you'd picture if you thought of the phrase *country life*. Mari laid on the horn. A house's front door swung open as she climbed out of the car.

"Darling, my dear, where have you been all my life?" a handsome man exclaimed, taking Mari into his arms and kissing her deeply. He was magazine-cover beautiful with dark hair and striking green eyes. They were the same height and build and fit perfectly together. Watching their love, I felt a momentary tug at my heart, mourning my lost marriage.

I noticed another man—larger but approximately the same age as the first one—had appeared in the doorway. Leaning against the doorframe in overalls, with no shirt underneath, he looked as if he was ready for a photo shoot. If I didn't know any better, I would have thought he was a model for Farmers Are Us. His nonchalant look was directed toward the lovers' embrace.

"Hey," Mari said to the man she'd kissed, "this is my new friend, Dacia. Dee, meet Mike and Mike. That guy," she said, pointing to the man on the stoop, "is Mike Pacheco. We call him Patch. And this one," she said as she looked at the man she held in her arms, "is mine." Her eyes met mine in a territorial stare. "As in *all mine*." I nodded as she released her boyfriend, turned, and stomped up the porch steps.

"Mike is fine," he said, holding his hand out for me to shake. "She's so possessive. Sorry."

"Mikey!" Mari called sharply, as if calling a dog. He turned and hustled in behind her.

Patch motioned with his head for me to come in. As I passed him, I heard an appreciative noise, so I glanced over my shoulder. "Great ass."

"Um, thanks? Can I use your bathroom?"

"Sure."

He showed me the door. As soon as I walked in, I glanced at the mirror to see if I looked as fucked up as I felt. The lines we had done had left me light-headed with a sense that I wasn't actually *in* my body. I washed my hands and took a few deep breaths before heading into the kitchen.

Sitting at the table, Mari had already poured out the baggie of drugs we'd got at the farm. I counted four one-inch lines on a small mirror in front of her. Mari did hers first and passed the straw to Mikey. When it was my turn, I snorted one. The effects were immediate: blood rushed between my ears, my nose burned, my eyes watered, and my stomach turned.

"Woo-hoo! Par-tay!" Patch hollered as he straightened up from doing his line. The room spun as I watched him, the movement glaring. He blinked back tears and smiled at me.

Mikey had moved into the kitchen area, where a large bottle of Patrón tequila sat next to the blender. He got busy blending drinks. Glancing around the room, I found a large wall clock that hung in the dining area; it was only eleven in the morning, and I immediately thought of Las Vegas. What would I have been doing had I flown there? Walking the Strip, watching the water fountain dance in front of the Bellagio, or window-shopping at the Fashion Show mall. I definitely wouldn't have been this fucked up. Mikey handed me a blended margarita.

"Cheers!" Mari toasted the three of us. Mikey bent down and kissed Mari as Patch wrapped his arm around me as if we'd been sweethearts for years.

We drank pitcher after pitcher of margaritas while we played cards, colored on a poster, and stacked dominoes. Patch had a glass steamroller pipe, and we smoked several bowls of his diggity. Even though I was drinking a lot, I didn't feel drunk, just high—really high because Mari kept putting little lines out on the mirror for us.

Mari seemed to melt into herself. She relaxed and smiled. The more I got to know her, the more I liked her. She was cute and smart and had a great sense of humor. Patch was growing on me too. He made me laugh so hard with his silly imitations of current film stars.

Time stood still as we smoked inside and outside. The backyard, still green for as late in the year as it was, featured a large wooden picnic table plus a horseshoe pit, and beyond that, farmland stretched out for miles.

Around dusk, we played several rounds of horseshoes, boys against girls. I was on one side with Patch, and Mikey and Mari were on the other side. When the sun slipped below the horizon, Mari and her man slipped into the house. I went to follow, but Patch stopped me.

"I'd stay and hang out here, if I were you. I promise you they want their privacy. Bumpin' uglies, you know?" He winked; I smiled.

Sitting on the edge of the table, he motioned for me to come closer. When I did, he wrapped his arms around my shoulders and legs around my waist. "Wanna fuck?"

My mouth fell open at his brazen statement, and assuming that to be an invitation, he leaned in and kissed me with passion, his tongue exploring my mouth, pulling me closer. My heart raced as his hands went down my back and cupped my butt. I almost couldn't help myself.

"You didn't answer my question," he mumbled as his hands found the waistband of my jeans. With deft fingers, he undid my pants and pulled them down to my knees. My breath quickened as he ran his hands under my shirt, finding my breasts.

Stepping out of my pants, I pulled off my shirt and climbed onto his lap. In response, he lowered his mouth to my bare chest. As he lay back on the table, I realized that for some odd reason, I had no qualms fucking this guy I had just met. I proceeded to undo the straps of his overalls and pulled them down. Nothing on underneath, with a shake, they fell onto my discarded clothes, and from nowhere, a condom appeared on his stiff penis. I climbed on and rode like I had never ridden a man before. Looking up at the night sky, I felt tiny yet all-powerful. The stars tilted and shifted above me as I came again and again.

We went to his room and had sex again, but this time, we had more tenderness between us. Afterward, he held me in his arms as we watched MTV's *Real World*. I didn't feel tired at all, which surprised me since I had consumed so much alcohol and smoked a ton of weed.

Around two in the morning, Patch dozed off, but unfortunately, I was wide-awake. Wrapping myself in a towel, I walked out to the backyard and then the living room to retrieve my clothes. I found the downstairs bathroom, which had a shower stall. I stepped in as the water was heating up but still chilly enough to make my nipples erect; the nerve endings of my skin were heightened, and I felt each drop fall separately. The shower stall seemed to shift under my feet when I moved my head, so I twisted back and forth to see how far the tiles would stretch. Nothing seemed real. Even the light seemed to glow brighter, and then dim, as if it were slowly breathing.

Eventually, the water became scalding, creating a sauna effect in the small bathroom. I breathed deeply, filling my lungs with the steam. Once I couldn't stand the heat anymore, I turned the water as cold as I could stand it, to the point that my teeth chattered. That left me feeling woozy and disconnected from my body, so I turned it hot again. Eventually, I turned the tap off and sat down on the tile floor. Even though the water wasn't on, tiny water droplets fell in rivulets down the shower door, making patterns. I thought of an aerial view of a large body of water, and each droplet was a boat; some moved fast while others were fat and slow.

A small knock on the door brought me out of my thoughts. "Yeah?"

Mari came in. I stood up in slow motion and grabbed a towel from the rack.

"There you are." She closed the door behind her and sat on the toilet as if it were a chair, holding a glass of orange liquid. "You bang Patch?"

"Yeah." My brain and mouth didn't seem to be completely connected. I managed to croak, "It was like fucking a tree."

"Excellent, my friend." She toasted her glass and took a sip. "He needed to get laid somethin' fierce. Condom, I hope?" I nodded. "Good. Appreciate you takin' one for the team."

I snorted the offering she had been working on and took a drink—a screwdriver. The orange juice was tangy in my mouth, and my body reacted to the natural sugar, giving me some energy. No wonder diabetics turned to fruit when their blood sugar slipped. My eyes focused like camera lenses, clear, blurry, clear. Mari was still talking to me, and I had to concentrate to catch what she was saying. "… and don't get too attached. He's somewhat of a player, you know?"

"Yeah," I said. The single syllable came out in a shallow breath.

"Let me know if you need anything." She winked and walked out.

CHAPTER 6

The hours blended together, and although I never slept, I eventually reconvened in the kitchen with the others about an hour before dawn. Mari gave me a large glass of orange juice. "With or without vodka?" I shook my head no; I didn't need any more alcohol. "Drink as much as you can. You need the vitamin C. Can you drink some water too?" I nodded, my mouth and brain refusing to coordinate.

Mikey made a pile of buttered toast, cut each piece into fours, and we all took several. Eating seemed to be a chore. Chewing specifically. When I swallowed, the ball of bread moved to my stomach as if it were forging the way for the first time.

Once I had finished the toast and drunk half the orange juice and all my water, Mari chopped up four more lines on the mirror and did hers first. Mikey went next, then Patch. My whole body quivered as they turned their attention to me, but I did the line anyway.

Within twenty seconds, I knew I was going to be sick. Feeling the bile creep up my throat, I ran to the bathroom just in time to vomit up my orange juice and bread balls. Mari appeared like a concerned mother, holding a glass of water and a piece of bread as I heaved another gutful of orange-flavored bile into the toilet. The back of my throat burned from the juice, my eyes watered, and my hands shook.

Mari handed me the bread. "See if you can keep that down. Let me know if you need anything else." She exited and closed the door behind her. I lowered myself to the floor and nibbled the bread. Once I was confident the bread would stay down, I got up and looked in the mirror at my ghastly reflection.

I ventured back to the kitchen after applying some makeup.

"Hey, look who's back!" Patch cried with elation when he saw me emerge from the bathroom. He pulled out the chair next to him and patted it. I obeyed as his thick arm encircled my shoulders, and I leaned into his solid mass. "You okay?" he asked with a gentleness I hadn't expected. I nodded and stared ahead, not focused on anything.

That day, we played more horseshoes, as well as liar's poker. Toward evening, Mari produced intricate coloring books along with several packs of colored pencils and markers. Long past midnight, we were still coloring. "What time do you gotta be at work tomorrow?" Mari asked. "Well, today, technically."

"One," I managed to say. My throat was dry, and my tongue felt two sizes too big for my mouth.

"Ah shit, that means I have to take you all the way to Oakland," she complained. I knew there were no nonstop flights from San Jose to Salt Lake. "It's cool, though," she continued. "You should get in at about eleven. That'll give you enough time to go home and dump off your stuff, right?" I nodded, engrossed with my coloring.

It seemed like only minutes had passed when Mari announced, "We should go soon. Are you all packed up?"

Walking on autopilot to the bathroom, I noticed the sun looked like it had been up a while. I changed into the cleanest clothes I had, applied some more makeup, shoved everything into my backpack, and zipped it up.

Patch kissed me with tenderness at the door. "Come on back now, ya hear?"

I nodded and forced a grin. Once I flopped into the passenger seat of Mari's car, I asked, "You okay to drive?"

"Of course," Mari replied as she pulled out of the driveway.

The drive to Oakland was like something out of a movie; the shadows didn't fit the objects creating them. Mari sang love songs from the radio and smiled and waved as she left me in front of terminal two.

Once I got through security and listed for standby, I sat close enough to hear my name when they called me. My eyes couldn't focus, and I didn't notice a blond-haired, blue-eyed man with a mustache sit next to me. It startled me when he spoke. "Salt Lake?" I nodded. "I'll save you a seat near the back, okay?" Since Morris Air didn't have seat assignments, passengers were able to sit anywhere. Standby folks usually ended up in the back anyway.

"Sure." It didn't seem like my voice. He patted my knee as he stood and got in line for the cattle-call boarding process.

There weren't many seats available, so I actually was relieved he had saved me a seat in the back of the plane. The middle seat wasn't taken in our row, so we had a little room. He introduced himself as Matt, and we made light conversation during takeoff.

Once the pilot announced the seat belt sign was turned off, the flight attendants began to take drink orders, and Matt leaned into me and asked, "Are you in the mile-high club?" I shook my head no. With that admission, he grabbed my wrist, pulled me into the small bathroom, pushed me up against the wall, and hissed into my ear, "Undo your pants if you want this."

I thought of Patch's big fingers undoing my jeans as I undid the button. Before I could unzip my fly, my pants were jerked to my knees, and Matt's cock entered me from behind as my breath blasted out of my lungs. Each syllable was a hard, forceful stroke. "Wel. Come. To. The. Mile. High. Club."

The door opened and closed, and he was gone. I stood there dumbfounded.

When I was left alone, feeling disoriented with my pants around my ankles, the door opened again. "Oh! Sorry, didn't know it was occupied!" a woman yelped as she pushed the door closed. I adjusted my pants and made a hasty exit.

As I made my way back to my seat, I saw there was no one in our row—Matt had disappeared. I glanced around and noticed a man's head in a middle seat close to the front. He was ducked low as if not to be noticed.

Taking the window seat, I shook my head. I huddled next to the window, pulled my jacket over my face, and fell into a deep sleep.

Before I knew it, the plane's wheels touching the runway woke me with a start. I pulled the jacket away from my face, looked out the window, and closed my eyes again. It would take a good fifteen minutes to get everyone off the plane.

I staggered to the bus stop to catch the long-term parking shuttle. For the second time that day, Matt saddled up next to me without me noticing. "I'd like to get to know you better," he said, "maybe party a little. You know what I mean?" I moved only my eyes in his direction. "I think you do know what I mean. You look high as hell," he said, chuckling, and held out a folded piece of paper. I took it and tucked it into the back pocket of my jeans. "Hope to hear from you soon," he said over his shoulder as he bolted across the street. I shook my head. I just wanted to lie down for a minute, close my eyes, and sleep.

Driving felt like a bad video game. The car seemed to lurch out of control as obstacles and traffic plotted against me. It took more effort than it should have, but then just staying awake had become a monumental task.

When I got to the house, it was already noon. Suzy heard me come in. Her head poked out of the kitchen, and she watched me climb the stairs with concern.

"You okay?" she called. I nodded and grunted but avoided looking at her.

When I reached my room, I fell onto the bed and called work. "I'm sick."

Then I slept for nineteen hours.

CHAPTER 7

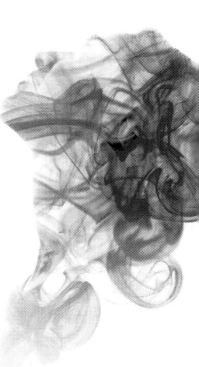

Since I mostly worked swing shifts, my bedtime fell somewhere between one and three in the morning. I couldn't tell you the last time I had been up at seven in the morning. I felt ravenous but otherwise no worse for wear.

The sun shone through a stained-glass skylight casting small rainbows over the plush green carpet. Casually, I walked down the staircase and entered the kitchen as if it were any regular day. Suzy's kids sat at the table, slurping cold cereal. I poured myself a cup of coffee as Suzy walked in, cloaked in her matching robe and fuzzy slippers.

"Hey. Are you feeling okay? You slept all day yesterday."

"Not all day."

"Vegas?"

"Salinas." She stared at me with her mouth pinched slightly, as if I were one of her kids and was about to get a lecture on manners. "It's the largest lettuce producer in the United States." I sipped my coffee, trying to remember what else Mari had told me about the little town.

"Lettuce?" She cocked one eyebrow, but I smiled and shrugged.

The kids finished their cereal and got ready for school. I took that as my cue to return to my room. When I got upstairs, I noticed I had two messages on my answering machine, but I didn't listen to either of them. I called Kris instead.

"What's up?" she asked, chipper and sharp.

"Me."

"Ha ha, you're funny," she deadpanned. "But really, why are you calling this early?"

"Did I wake you up?"

"No, of course not."

"Okay." I paused. "Um, can I come by before work? I have a shitload to tell you about my weekend."

"Vegas?" I heard her curiosity come to life. "What'd you do?"

I laughed. "Not Vegas, and not what I did, but *who* I did."

"No kidding? Yeah, I want to hear, so stop by. Laura goes to preschool in about a half hour."

"Cool beans. See you in a bit."

I hung up and pushed play on the answering machine and listened to the first message.

"Tuesday, 7:48 p.m.," the automated voice announced. Then I heard a voice that surprised me. "Hey, Dacia." It was Christopher from the bar. "I'm down here at City Limits. If you're around, stop by." I pushed delete and played the next message. The automated voice announced, "Wednesday, 1:11 a.m." It was Christopher again, and this time, he sounded drunk. "Hey, sexy," he slurred. "Where you at? It's dull when you're not here. Come down—" Another voice interrupted him in the background. "Dude, don't whine." I recognized it as Cory, who must've taken the pay phone away from Christopher.

Damn it! Men! I was getting laid plenty, and Christopher was going to ruin a good friendship if he pushed this shit. I thought of the two guys I was sleeping with—I couldn't do three. Plus, I wasn't into guys shorter than me—period.

As I deleted the second message, I realized that over the course of one weekend, I had doubled the number of men I had slept with. Leonard would have called me a slut. I shook my head to get rid of the ex-husband thoughts.

While in the shower, I mulled over how I could tell Christopher I wasn't interested in him. More important, I wasn't sexually attracted to him. That was the real kicker. I decided to focus on how much his friendship meant to me, but I knew I had to get that across without sounding condescending. In the worst-case scenario, I could just explain that I was already seeing someone—like Patch, or Matt. *Matt Patch*—that made me giggle as a cartoon of a patch on a doormat floated into my mind.

Thinking of Matt, I went to find the jeans with his phone number tucked in the back pocket. My entire floor was covered in clothes, so it took a minute to find the number. I called and left him a message with my number. "It was," I said and hesitated, "interesting to meet you. Call me sometime."

When I got to Kris's house, she was still in her bathrobe, just finishing her first pot of coffee. Thankfully, there was no dress code at work, and most of the time, I rolled in wearing sweats with no makeup. Suffice it to say, getting ready for work was a breeze, and at least I didn't make her feel out of place by being more dressed up.

"So, you fucked both of them?" she asked in utter surprise when I finished my weekend tale. "Did you use a condom?"

I took a sip of the sweet, white coffee Kris had set in front of me. "With Patch, yeah, but not the airplane dude. But I don't think he finished, you know?"

"Girl, be careful," she warned, but I heard the envy in her voice.

When I got to work that day, I sat in my normal cubicle. Joy eventually showed up, clocked in, and sat down next to me. Despite her sweet, grandma-like smile, I couldn't make eye contact with her. I felt like she could see right through me. Now that I wasn't high with a full quart of alcohol in me, I definitely felt a little slutty, not to mention that I'd also burned one of my sick days sleeping off the side effects of being high.

As we started taking calls, Joy stood behind me and rubbed my neck and shoulders as if I had a personal masseuse. "Thank you for calling Morris Air." We said it in unison this time, but when not in unison, it sounded like we were chanting the phrase in a round.

Joy had to stop massaging my shoulders when one of us had to write a ticket. "I'm a licensed massage therapist," she whispered, "*and* a healer." She touched my necklace, rotating the stone in her fingers. I protectively covered it with my hand. "Seriously," she said between calls, "make an appointment to come see me."

Around three in the afternoon, Mari came in and took the cubicle on the other side of the partition across from me. I heard her log in and begin to take calls. "Thank you for calling Morris Air. How may I help you?"

On my first break, I slipped her a note, asking her the time of her scheduled break. The scribbled note I got back read, *@ my car, 5:30, south parking lot.*

At five thirty, I headed out and found Mari already in her car. I slid into the passenger side and noticed the CD case with two small lines.

"Thought you might need this today," she said, handing me a rolled bill. I took it all up one nostril without a thought. My eyes burned and watered.

"Thanks. Got any more I could take home?"

"Um," she hesitated, looking out the window away from me. "Gotta charge ya."

"Yeah, of course," I responded, even though that hadn't crossed my mind. I fumbled for my purse. "I've got twenty on me."

She nodded, opened the center console, and grabbed a bit of plastic tied into a knot. "Coincidentally, here's a twenty-sack." She held it out to me. "You caught it before I stomped it, so it's clean."

"Okay." I had no idea what she was talking about.

She got out of the car without another word. I followed her, and we walked back to the building. As we rounded the west side, I reached into my front pocket and took out a twenty-dollar bill. Glancing up, I saw Joy in the window, looking down at us with curiosity. Her eyes narrowed when I handed Mari the money, but I played it off and waved at her with a bit of arrogance. This drug made me so bold.

We entered through the lobby, and as we took the stairs up to our cubicles, my heart rate increased as my hands got moist. That teeny-tiny amount I did had me high as a kite.

"The second half of your shift is gonna fly by," Mari promised, giving me a little wink. "Don't forget to hydrate!" I laughed at her as if we had an inside joke.

Joy clocked out when I clocked in, refusing to look at me, and when she returned from her lunch break, she didn't give me my massage like earlier. Her energy toward me had changed. But I didn't care—I was feeling fine, and as promised, the second half of my shift did fly by.

Right before I clocked out, I penned Mari a note, telling her I would be at City Limits when she got off work. On my way out, I stopped by the phone bank to call Kris.

"Hey," I said when she answered.

"What's up?"

"Got some of that stuff I told you about. I'm gonna head to the bar."

"Okay. I'll leave the kid with Dave for an hour or so. See you down there," she promised. I practically danced out the door.

CHAPTER 8

I immediately saw Christopher when I walked in. The band was playing loud and out of key, the atmosphere dank and smoke filled. The lights from the bar mimicked the lighting from a movie or television commercial, highlighting his facial features. His jet-black hair tumbled down his back in big smooth waves, and I noticed a dimple just above the corner of his upturned mouth. It was sad, but I was totally *not* interested.

I had helped myself to a little line on the way to the bar, and my feet felt like they weren't working. I floated over to the stool next to Christopher and sat down.

"What's up, cutie-pie?" I shouted in Christopher's ear.

"Hey, hot stuff!" His eyes lit up, and he threw his arms around me in a huge hug. We were almost the same height when sitting on bar stools. He motioned for the bartender. Doc recognized me and knew what I was drinking—a Cape Cod with extra lime.

"How you been? I've missed you," Christopher asked with his boy-next-door smile.

"Good," I said without commenting on the "missed you." Kristine showed up, and Doc brought my drink and took her order.

"Check it out! I'm in a Chris sandwich," I said, laughing when he returned with her cocktail. Doc and Kris looked at me with a mix of curiosity and patience. "Chris and Kris," I said, rotating my thumb from left to right as a fit of giggles overtook me.

"Gotcha," Doc said, returning his attention to another patron.

"You're cute," Christopher said as he took a swig of his beer.

"No, she's not," Kris interjected. "She's drunk and annoying." I started giggling again.

When the first round was empty, I looked at Kris, motioning to the ladies' room. We headed to the bathroom and squeezed into a stall. I grabbed the knotted plastic and the cap of a pen out of my little handbag. Kris got a pile on the end of the pen cap and snorted it. Her eyes watered immediately as her face turned several shades of red. "Holy shit."

"Right?" I said, taking a nose hit myself. Instantly, I felt more in control of my mouth. My spine felt straighter; my toes tingled.

"Split that with me?" Kris asked.

"Just have it," I answered. "Mari should be by in an hour or so. I bet she has more." Kris nodded, putting the wadded-up plastic into her wallet, and we rejoined Christopher.

When our third round of drinks was over, Mari showed and sat on the far side of Christopher. We ordered another round. Before the drinks arrived, she motioned for me to follow her to the bathroom.

"I'm not staying long; did you want more of that shit before I stomp it?" she asked.

"Um, I guess."

"Here, I'll front it to you. Just pay me next week or whenever, okay?" I nodded and took another bindle from her.

When we returned to the bar, Mari took her glass and swallowed the whole thing in one long drink. "Gotta be gettin' home." She smiled, winking in my direction. I didn't realize she hadn't paid for her cocktail until after she was gone. Doc put it on my tab.

Throughout the night, Kris and I went into the bathroom and did bumps of the yellowish powder off the pen cap. When we returned right before last call, Christopher looked to Kris. "You should tell your friend to go out with me."

"She's a big girl. She can decide who she goes out with," Kris answered, an edge to her voice. She turned to me. "You should go out with this guy. He's kinda cute." Doc set another round in front of us as I prepared myself to let him down gently.

"You're sweet," I said to Christopher as I made myself comfortable on the bar stool between them. He smiled and wiggled his eyebrows at me, the side dimple creasing. "Maybe."

"Progress," Christopher said to himself, taking a long swallow from his fresh drink.

"I think I'm heading home," Kris announced as she slid her half-full glass toward me and gathered her things. "See ya mañana, chica," she said and kissed my cheek.

Christopher and I stayed until the bar's lights came on and we got thrown out. He walked me to my car.

"You okay to drive?" he asked. "My house is a block away if you want to come sober up there for an hour or two."

"Naw, I'm good," I said, unlocking my car door.

"Well, okay," he said, crestfallen. "Buckle up and drive safe."

As I got into the car, his eyes dropped to my legs and then meandered back up to my chest. Desire creased his face as our eyes met.

"Thanks. See you around," I said unceremoniously as I closed the door and started the engine. Christopher crossed to the opposite side of the street and disappeared into the shadows.

It was only a two-and-a-half-mile drive home, but it seemed ten times that. At one point, the lights from a police car in front of me reminded me that I was over the legal blood alcohol limit. My stomach squeezed into a knot, and for a moment, I thought I'd be sick. The feeling passed as I drove by the cop, grateful he'd found someone else to harass.

Relief washed over me as I pulled up to the house I called home. I took a few deep breaths in order to steady my legs enough to walk from the car to the house.

Once inside, I heard every shift and groan of the wooden stairs as I ascended to my room. I closed my bedroom door and stashed the little baggie of chunky powder under my bed. There really wasn't that much left. I would save it for work.

After I lay down, my mind continued to spin—I was wide-awake. Might as well make use of the extra energy. I rearranged the books on the shelf and sorted the ankle-deep clothes across the floor into colored piles to be washed, and as I checked the pockets, I found a five-dollar bill. When my room was spotless, I took a shower.

The small bathroom filled up with steam, and I let the water pour over me until it grew cold. Stepping out of the shower, I sat on the toilet lid and watched the steam stream out of the window in ribbons. When my body temperature started to lower, I sprinted from the bathroom back to my room to put on warm pajamas. I looked at the clock—4:20 a.m. For some unexplainable reason, that made me giggle.

As I smoked a bowl, I lay there watching the shadows on the ceiling move with cars from the street below. The shadows moved like line dancers, swaying diagonally from left to right. Even though my body felt exhausted, my mind was cranked on high.

I eventually heard the sounds of the morning rituals—the clank and clatter of cereal bowls as the kids got ready for school; the back door opening and closing for Sparky, their Sheltie, to go out and do his morning business; the squeal of the bus brakes; the kids scrambling and hollering their farewells; and Suzy getting ready for work, but even still, sleep didn't come.

I hauled my exhausted body out of bed around noon and threw on a pair of sweats. Suzy was waiting for me at the bottom of the stairs.

"Good morning, girl," she said sweetly, but her eyes hard, "or afternoon?" I shrugged and went to move around her. She sidestepped and blocked my exit. "You can't smoke weed in the house." Her tone was flat, the hardness matching her stare.

"I don't know what you're talking about." My eyes stayed on the floor. I'm a terrible liar.

"I can smell it! The *kids* can smell it! And whatever other drugs you're doing, stop. Not in *this* house."

"I wasn't, I haven't—" My sleep-deprived brain couldn't form the sentences.

"Well, don't!" she snapped and turned on her heels, marching into the kitchen. "I don't need the money *that* bad," she said over her shoulder with a sarcastic edge.

I highly doubted that statement. *Who does she think she is?* I fumed as I stomped to my car. *Your landlord,* my brain echoed back.

CHAPTER 9

Mari and I orchestrated our schedules by doing some shift trades so that we had four days off together. We met at the airport in Salt Lake and flew standby to San Jose. Freddie stayed in the trunk once again. We stopped for Coke and Captain Morgan at the same C store, and while I mixed the drinks, Mari rummaged around in the center console and found the plastic baggie.

"Here's a bit. See if you can scrape it to get us a couple little lines. I usually leave more for the return attitude adjustment. Sorry."

"No worries." I slit the plastic with care and scraped the contents onto a CD case.

Once crushed, it had enough for two bitty lines. I did mine first and held the rolled-dollar straw and CD up to Mari's nose. Going seventy-five miles an hour and never taking her hands off the steering wheel, she snorted it and chased it down with a strong Coke and rum.

When we got to the big farm, we found Mari's supply man lounging in the shade, smoking a cigarette with no one else around. The man got up and smiled—it was a menacing smile. Mari's mouth went slack.

"Finish your drink, and come with me," she instructed as I gave her a funny look. "Seriously, don't make me do this alone." She got out and looked over her shoulder. "Leave your morals in the car."

Taking two big gulps of the sweet drink, I gathered my courage and followed her. Mari switched effortlessly to Spanish and spoke to the man. He answered, and although I had no idea what they were saying, the look on his face made me nervous; there was too much sexual energy in his upturned mouth.

"Follow my lead," Mari whispered as we trailed the man into one of the metal buildings. It was cooler inside, but not by much. The stagnant air smelled of fertilizer.

Without warning, Mari took off her shirt. I watched as the man grabbed her boobs with both hands and buried his face between them, and then, reaching down between her legs, he used one hand to fondle her through her jeans. He pulled away from her, and my eyes grew wide in horror as he licked his lips and moved toward me, rubbing the growing bulge in his pants.

As I stood there speechless, he grabbed my shirt and yanked it over my head. It happened so fast I couldn't even stop it. His eyes lit up when he realized I wasn't wearing a bra. Like a snake's mouth, his mouth darted and took in one of my nipples as he pressed his hard penis against my thigh.

"Just roll with it," Mari whispered, one hand covering her eyes.

I noticed she had put her shirt back on. The man pulled back and handed me my shirt as he spoke to Mari in Spanish—*muy bueno* was all I understood. As he handed Mari something, he turned to me and placed a package in my hand. Mari was already at the door.

"Come on, Dee. Hurry." Her voice sounded urgent.

When we drove off, the wheels would have squealed if we'd been on asphalt.

"Do me up a big one." She breathed, slamming the remains of her cocktail. I began to open the package the man had given me. "He gave you one too?" she asked.

"Yeah."

As if a light switch had been thrown, her mood and attitude switched. "Oh my god! That worked out better than I expected!" She huffed the large line I gave her as she drove with her knee. "Do you have any idea how much money you can make with that shit?"

"Um." I looked at the package. "No, not really."

"Well, grasshopper, you're gonna find out." She winked.

The weekend with Mike and Patch played out just like the previous one, except we went out on a good old-fashioned double date. Since we were all high as hell, we skipped dinner and went to see *The Fugitive*.

The smells of the theater made me nauseated. The smells of popcorn, nachos with jalapeños, pizza, and sweaty people didn't mix well, and I cupped my hands over my face to reduce the all-encompassing fumes. It was literally the first movie I'd ever seen where I didn't eat a huge tub of buttered popcorn. *This is ridiculous,* I thought. *A movie with no popcorn is sacrilege. I've got to quit this shit,* I heard my inner voice request. *Done,* I replied to myself. *This is the last weekend I'm coming out here with Mari.* Shame washed over me as I thought of our stop at the farm that morning. I forced myself to focus on Harrison Ford and quiet my conscience.

After the show, we found a local bar and closed it down, playing pool and swilling pitchers of beer. Mari and I went to the ladies' room together to do more lines of meth. The meth was definitely heavier than coke. More of a yellowish-brown color, it lacked the nice, numbing effect that cocaine offered—all my senses were on overload, not just my ability to smell. Every shadow and detail got my attention. And it certainly affected my appetite. In less than two weeks, I had lost eight pounds.

"Just one of the upsides," Mari commented when I'd showed her the belt I had to wear.

Throughout the weekend, Patch and I fell into a routine. We established which side of the bed we would lounge on while watching MTV, and a pattern of who'd roll the next joint. I left my stuff in his room instead of leaving it in the guest bathroom, and we had sex often. Sometimes we used a condom; sometimes we didn't, but I felt I could justify this since I was on the pill.

After four days of no sleep, no food, and mass quantities of alcohol, Mari stopped at a Walgreens and bought a CoverGirl loose-powder compact on our way back to the airport. When we got back in the car, she opened the compact and dumped out the contents.

"Where's your shit?" she demanded.

Confused, I pulled out the bindle of meth I still had and handed it to her. She opened it, dumping the contents into the powder compact.

"It's so you don't get caught." She handed the compact to me, rummaged around in her large bag, found a similar-looking powder compact, and filled it up as well. "I've never had a problem, but you never know." Her eyes looked tired. It made me wonder if I looked as drained.

At the airport, my heart raced as my bag went through the x-ray machine. I glanced around, looking for drug-sniffing dogs, but saw only TSA agents. "Not even real cops," Mari whispered in my ear.

By the time I retrieved my bags, my hands were shaking as my eyes darted wildly around at the airport workers and other passengers. Even though no one was looking at me, I felt like I was on center stage—I was guilty, and everyone would figure me out.

CHAPTER 10

When I got back home, I had nine messages on my answering machine. I peeled off my clothes as I listened to them. The first and third messages were from Kris, saying that she and Dave wanted more of "that great lettuce from Salinas."

The second and ninth messages were from Christopher. In his first message, he apologized for calling so late on Saturday, and his second message was another drunk late-night call from the pay phone at the club.

The other five messages were from Matt. The first one was a normal "call me" type of message, but in the second message, his request for me to call him seemed a bit more urgent. By the third message, he sounded irritated, and in the fourth message, he sounded downright angry that I hadn't called him back yet. In the fifth and final one, he basically told me if I didn't call him within the next twenty-four hours, we were through. So much for being fuck friends. The machine announced the last message had been recorded fourteen hours ago, so I dialed his number. After four rings, it went to the machine.

"Hey, Matt. It's me, Dacia. Sorry I didn't call sooner. I was out of town. Call me back. I'll make it up to you." I hung up as my body relaxed into the carpet.

Just as I started to drift off, the phone rang, and my heart kick-started so fast I thought I was having a heart attack. At that point, I wasn't sure whether my physical reaction was due to a lack of food and sleep or due to the drugs, but it was probably both.

"Hi, babe." Matt's voice was cheerful, lacking any apparent sign of frustration or anger.

"Hey." I seriously needed to eat, or sleep. Or both. As I lay there, I reached out for my backpack, rummaging around for the small package of peanuts I'd got from the stewardess on the flight going to San Jose—I remembered I'd tucked it into the front zipper pocket. After a bit of digging, I pulled the peanuts out.

"Can I come over tonight after you get off work? I miss you."

"Um, I guess," I agreed, even though the phone felt like it weighed ten pounds and my head felt as if it weighed fifty. I could barely lift it from the carpet. My body seemed to mold to the floor. "I gotta go, though."

I thought I heard him say, "Love ya," or something along those lines as I dropped the receiver into the cradle, but I really couldn't be sure since my brain felt unplugged from my body.

Holding the peanuts, I finally managed to open them and chew the first one. The peanut turned to paste, peanut butter without the sugar. I put the second one in my mouth and sucked it for a minute before starting the chewing process. When I was done with the package, I fell into a deep sleep.

The squeal of bus brakes brought me out of my slumber; it was like an alarm clock. My body jerked—the sensation you get when you dream you're falling but you wake up before hitting the ground. Unsure exactly what had woken me up, I rolled my head to the side and looked at the clock radio. It read 3:23 p.m. I was supposed to have been at work at one. Dialing the phone, I formulated my lie. "I've been at the ER since about five this morning," I heard myself say. "Yes, I'm fine but had no way to make a phone call." The lies became easier. "I'll be there in fifteen minutes."

Getting up, I was able to move much faster since I'd slept for five hours. As I sat on the edge of the bed, my stomach grumbled. Food. I needed food, so there was no time for a shower. I tried to remember when I had showered last. The last time I had showered was with Patch. Had that been yesterday? Or the day before? Or the day before that? My thoughts drudged through the fog in my brain, trying to connect the dots of my life. I rubbed deodorant under each armpit and threw on some clean clothes. On the way to work, I swung through McDonald's and ordered a large fries and a vanilla shake. The sweet and salty mix was perfect for my empty stomach.

The company allowed me to swap my shift, so I had to stay until one in the morning or else get docked in my personnel file. The company did that for medical emergencies like the one I had reported earlier.

Once off and home, I trudged up to my room. I felt like I was walking through quicksand. I just needed sleep. But when I turned on my bedroom light,

Matt was there, lying on my bed. I let out a high-pitched scream, totally forgetting that he'd asked to come by.

"Where've you been?" he asked.

"Work."

"I thought you usually get off at eleven—it's after one!" His voice was just this side of aggressive.

"How the fuck did you get in here?"

"I watched how the kids got in after school and found the key when the house went dark. Then I just snuck in. That dog only barked once—what a worthless piece of shit, huh? I could have murdered the kids and raped your roommate."

"You're fucking creepy." I dropped my purse and took off my shoes.

"You get more of that shit while you were out of town?"

"Maybe."

"You got more. C'mon, hook me up, and I'll leave. You sure you don't want a little?" He smiled and kissed me lightly as he caressed my back.

"Sleep. I need sleep." His kisses became more fevered as he pulled at my sweats.

"I know something else you need," he mumbled as he kissed my neck and stroked my inner thighs.

"Okay," I conceded. "One bump and then you go." I pulled away from him and retrieved my purse from the floor. After dumping it out, I found the little knotted plastic.

"What do you want for the whole thing?" he asked, and I looked at him in confusion. "I'll give you a hundred bucks for all of it."

I shook my head no, remembering Mari had said there was enough there to equal a week's worth of work.

"Five hundred," I insisted.

"Oh, you are high," he said, snorting the line I'd made for him. As I did a much smaller line, my thoughts cleared instantly, and I no longer felt the need to sleep. In fact, I felt fine. "So why don't you come with me to a little party at my friend Walt's house," he suggested, and after a moment's thought, I agreed.

The party was still going hard when we got there at about two in the morning. Smoke—cigarette mixed with marijuana—clouded the room. People crammed together on the crushed-velvet couch. More people lined the hallway that went into the kitchen. "Daughter" by Pearl Jam blasted over the radio. I got a beer and looked around. I noticed one other female besides me and about a dozen men. Matt pulled me into the bedroom, asking if we could do a line with his friends.

"Um, I've got to sell this and make some money off it," I told him.

"Oh, babe, you know I'll take care of you!"

He took the bindle from my hands and, untying it, poured half onto a mirror.

He chopped it into five large lines. People came and went as I sat on the bed. Once we were alone, I noticed more than half the meth was gone.

"Hey, what about me?" I asked indignantly.

"Oh, sorry, I didn't know you wanted one."

"It's my shit," I said, scooping out a pile for myself as he looked at me curiously. "What?"

"Well, I have a fantasy I want to tell you about. You game?" he asked, his eyes dancing devilishly.

"Sure." I huffed a large line—it made me gag.

"Come on then," Matt said and grabbed my hand.

Leading me into the bathroom, he turned on the bathtub faucet, filled the tub, and told me to take off my clothes, which I did. He proceeded to bathe me and to shave my legs and pussy, all while telling me that I was sexy and beautiful. It was erotic, and I got wet just watching him shave my most private parts. When he was done, he carried me into the bedroom, gently laid me on the bed, kissing my breasts and stomach, and moved lower. "Ready for the fantasy?"

I was confused, thinking what we'd just done in the bathtub *was* the fantasy, but I'd failed to notice pairs of handcuffs he held in his hands. My breath caught in my throat at what came next. As he secured my outstretched arms to the bed's headboard, he used a belt from a bathrobe to secure my right leg to the bed's footboard, leaving my other leg free.

"I want to watch you fuck my friends," he said so matter-of-factly that it caught me off guard.

"What do you mean?" Panic took root in my gut.

"Don't worry. No one will hurt you. It's just Walt and maybe someone else; I don't know. I think I'll go out and ask who wants to fuck you."

"What are you talking about?" I didn't like this. I squirmed, looking at the bonds holding me in place. Panic lurched from my gut to my chest, swelling up in waves.

"Don't worry. I'll be right here." He grabbed a condom from the nightstand and placed it on my stomach. "I'm gonna watch; I told you that."

He placed another condom next to the first and started toward the door and then paused. He walked back to me, bent down and kissed me gently on the mouth, and placed two more condoms on my stomach.

CHAPTER 11

Needless to say, I didn't get any sleep that night, and although I made it to work on time, my supervisor took one look at me and told me I should probably take a sick day.

"I feel fine," I lied.

"You look like ass," she snapped, placing her hand on my forehead. "You don't have a fever, but are you sure you're okay? Your coloring isn't right."

Dishonesty seemed to be a new talent I had discovered. "Oh, I just got some bad news today; that's all." I made my expression sad and pouty. "Good friend, cancer." I turned away and put my hand to my mouth—an Emmy Award–winning moment, for sure.

"Oh, I'm so sorry to hear that," my supervisor tsked. "Well, there are plenty of sick days available. Maybe you should take one and go be with her." I nodded a reply.

Once home, I walked back up the stairs as Suzy asked me if I was all right. "Just a little tired," I explained with a weak smile. I fell onto the bed and went to sleep right away.

The shrill screech of bus brakes and the front door opening and closing woke me, that alarm clock that told me it was twentyish after three. Two hours of sleep. I rolled over and put my blanket over my head just as my phone rang. I answered against my better judgment.

"Oh wow, I wasn't expecting you to answer," Kris greeted me when I mumbled a hello into the receiver.

"Sick," I grunted.

"Oh, I'm sorry. Anything I can do for you?"

"No, it's cool. I don't think I'm *sick-sick*. I just need sleep."

"Well, rest up. Dave and I have a date tonight, and I thought we'd stop by when you got off work. But since you're off, could we stop by a little earlier?"

"Um, sure," I agreed, my voice weak with fatigue.

"Perfect. See you in a bit!" Her voice was peppy and borderline obnoxious. I went back to sleep.

A noise outside my bedroom door brought me to consciousness. Had it been a few minutes or a few hours? I heard Suzy talking, although it was muffled. "I'm not sure she's feeling well."

Kris's muffled voice floated through the crack of my open door. "Oh, she won't mind. We told her we were stopping by." My door opened, and a stream of light shot through the room toward the bed. I sat up and switched on the lamp by my bed, wondering what time it was.

"Hey," Kris whispered. Dave followed her into my room and closed the door behind them. I heard Suzy's footsteps retreat down the stairs. "You okay?" she asked me, and I nodded. "We were hoping to get a little of that shit," she said, helping herself to a bowl of marijuana on my dresser.

"I'm not supposed to smoke in here anymore," I mumbled. "Open the window at least."

She did and blew the hit out into the night air. "Where's the glue?"

"It's in the little wooden box over there." I finally sat up in bed, yawned, and pointed across the room. I listened to her rummage around and heard the familiar noise of her crushing up the rocks and chopping them on a mirror. Instantly, I was awake, my body craving the powder.

I did a line, took a hit from the pipe, and sat back down on my bed. The drugs woke me up as they wiggled into my bloodstream, pushing their way to my brain. Kris sat next to me on the bed and put her hand on my knee. With one eyebrow cocked, I looked at her, questioningly.

"We want to make you feel better." She slid off the bed and knelt between my legs.

"What the hell are you doing?" I asked as I noticed her husband taking off his clothes.

"Making you feel better," she insisted as she untied the string of my pajama bottoms. "Lay back, and don't worry about anything."

Confusion washed over me as her husband gently nudged me to lie down as Kris's small hands manipulated me between my legs. Then came the sensation of her soft mouth licking me. I couldn't help but be turned on. Her husband, completely naked now, straddled my chest, and I took his penis in my mouth as Kris pulled off my pajama pants and fingered me with gusto.

Around midnight, we were spent, sprawled across my bed. Kris's husband went to the bathroom. "I can't believe I just fucked your husband."

"Yeah, and it was awesome." Her voice lilted, a songlike quality to it. "We've got to run, though. I told the sitter we'd be home by now. Mind if I take a bit of that shit?"

"I've got to charge you. Sorry." I sounded like Mari.

"No worries. Put it on my tab, and let me know what I owe you on payday, okay?" She got up and started to dress just as Dave came back in. He pulled his pants on over his BVDs.

I got up and, wrapping myself in a little blanket, surveyed how much meth I had left. Mari and I had planned on going back to San Jose on our next days off, but that was still a week away. I split what was there and let Kris think I was giving her half of what I had, even though I had more stashed in my sock drawer.

"Forty cool?" I asked.

She looked at the pile I had scraped for her. "Forty?"

I nodded. "It's a front and all I have," I lied.

"Fine," she agreed, pulling a small vial from her bag. I scraped the powder into her little container. "Thanks, my friend," she said and kissed me lightly on the cheek before they left.

Even though it was after midnight, I scraped the rest from the mirror, did a small bump, and called Matt. "Last call?" I asked him.

"Be there in fifteen," he said without asking me any other details.

Using one hand to run a brush through my hair and the other to brush my teeth, I hurried to get ready. I threw on a denim skirt and simple button-down blouse, and for makeup, I swiped one coat of clear lip gloss across my lips and threw a hint of mascara on my lashes. No one would notice I hadn't completely done up my face.

Christopher was in his normal spot at the end of the bar. Desperate to avoid him, I blended into the crowd and slipped into a corner booth.

Before I ordered my drink, I saw Matt scanning the room for me. I motioned for him and cringed, hoping Christopher hadn't noticed. Sauntering over to my table, Matt stopped a waitress and ordered drinks before sliding in next to me.

"Just get off?" he asked.

"In more ways than one," I teased, taking a sip of the drink that had just been placed in front of me. He looked at me with puzzlement. "I just fucked my best friend's husband," I revealed, watching his face for a reaction.

"She's not going to be too happy about that," he deadpanned.

"Wrong. She was there, an active participant."

A wide smile spread across his face. "She lick you?"

"Yep."

"You lick her?" I nodded again. "That's hot," he said, taking a long drink of his beer. "I'm getting hard just thinking about it."

I nodded, listening to the last song the band was playing, when, without warning, Matt grabbed me by the wrist and yanked me out of the booth. He pulled me to the door and outside.

"What the fuck—"

Before I could finish my sentence, he pushed me through the bushes that lined the front of the club.

"What are you—"

Cupping his hand over my mouth, he cut me off and used his other hand to reach under my skirt. He pulled my panties aside and plunged his erection into me. I could hear people walking on the sidewalk just a few feet from us. My heart raced as Matt rammed his cock into me hard; one hand still covered my mouth as he pressed my head against the wall of the building.

"I want to watch your friend lick you," he hissed into my ear. "I want to watch her watching her husband fuck you. Then I want you to watch me fuck her." His voice was ragged, lost in passion.

My mind reeled at this as I heard people walking out of the club—their slurred goodbyes, laughter, and more conversations all around us. The bar was closing, and I couldn't help but wonder if Christopher had left already.

Matt released his hand from my mouth, and as I breathed in, I had an orgasm—my eyes pinched tight as colors exploded behind my eyelids. As Matt reached his climax, he buried his face in my neck. His warm breath hit my shoulder as he continued to relay his X-rated fantasies to me.

When I finally opened my eyes, I was staring directly at Christopher, peering at us through the bushes. My body jumped as recognition washed over Christopher's expression. When Christopher realized I had seen him, his eyes blazed with disappointment. He slowly shook his head and walked away.

CHAPTER 12

The next few days were uneventful. Work, meth buzz till dawn, a few hours of sleep, and back to work. Mari and I did bumps on our lunch breaks, so the drugs always started before my shifts ended.

One Thursday after work, I found only one message on my answering machine: Kristine wanting more of the sickly powder. I told her my prices had to go up because I was almost out, when, in reality, I had plenty to last me until my days off. I just needed to replace the money I had given Mari, or else I'd be short on my rent.

Thursday was ladies' night at the club, and I traded my shift each week so that I could be off by ten that night. It was a night I never missed; drinks were half-price, and most nights, so many men were there that I never paid for my drinks—half-price or not.

That particular Thursday, I found Christopher at his normal spot. Half of me wanted to disappear into the crowd, and the other half of me craved a normal night. I walked up to the bar and sat next to Christopher. "Fuck off," he said, not looking at me.

"What?" I asked, motioning for Doc to get me a drink.

"Really?" he asked. "I call you and invite you to meet me here, but you say you're sick. Then I see you fucking some other dude in the bushes as I'm leaving." He took a long pull from his beer. "Is this the only club in town where you can get your rocks off, Dacia? I mean, really ..." I had completely forgotten he had called earlier that night.

"Sorry," I mumbled, picking up my drink to leave. He twisted in his seat and blocked my escape.

"One date. That's all I'm asking for." His eyes bore into mine, ice-cold, and his tone sounded like we should be at the negotiating table of some corporate office. He continued. "Let me show you how you should be treated for one night. If it's not magical, if you don't have fun, if the company is boring and stale and you're counting the minutes till it's over, I'll leave you alone. We'll just be friends. But at least give me one night to prove to you your worth." My throat had tightened, and I felt trapped. I shrugged, nodded, and took a drink of my cocktail. "When?" he asked, his voice stern and expectant.

"Can I wear high heels?"

"You're that concerned about my height?" he asked and chuckled, swallowing his beer. "Wear the tallest ones in your closet."

"Really?"

"Yeah," he insisted.

"Okay. Um … I have plans on my next days off," I said weakly. "The weekend after that?"

"Two weeks?" he asked incredulously. "You're going to make me wait two weeks? Are you worth it?" I rolled my eyes, sighed, and nodded. He lifted his drink to tap mine. "I'm sure you are. It's a date."

"It's a date."

As I walked away, I noticed him suppressing a smile. One date. I could go out with a guy over four inches shorter than me on one date night. At least he was handsome. Maybe he could wear platform shoes. The image made me giggle.

I slipped out right before last call.

I found Kris sitting on my porch when I got home. "Hey." She sounded as if she had been crying.

"Hey." I sat next to her on the top step. "You okay?"

She shook her head. "Dave's freaking about you."

"Me?" I asked incredulously, and she nodded.

"He's getting all possessive about you and getting all aggressive with me. He's just getting all weird and shit. I don't know." Tears glistened on her bottom lids. I pulled my pipe from my purse and handed it to her. She took a long draw from it and handed it back. "He wants to know who you're fucking and when you're coming over. He wants to fuck you again."

"Duh," I said playfully. She laughed as tears spilled down her face.

"You got any more of that shit?" she asked, taking another hit from the pipe. I put my arm around her. I remembered that I'd already told her I had run out, so I wasn't sure how to answer her.

"Um … let's go up and check," I replied, getting to my feet.

When we walked into my room, I flipped the light on, and Kris shrieked in surprise. Matt was there, naked on my bed.

"Dude, what are you doing? You can't keep doing this!" My voice was much louder than I had intended. I certainly didn't want to wake Suzy.

He sat up and smiled. Kris stared at him, which made him hard. "This is *that* friend? Oh my god! Is tonight my lucky night?" Matt exclaimed, his eyes dancing.

"Oh shit, this is *that* guy?" Kris said. "The mile-high dude?"

"Oh, my reputation precedes me, I see," he said, cozying up to her and sliding his arms around her waist from behind. He started to kiss her neck.

"Um, hello, I'm married," she protested. But when he unbuttoned her jeans and dipped his hand in, she moaned in response, making no effort to move away.

"Married or not, you're wet as fuck. Come on over here, Dacia, and show me how you lick your best friend." He peeled her jeans and panties down to her ankles, and she leaned her head back onto his shoulder, allowing him to caress her breasts. "C'mon now," he indicated to me again. "Kneel down right here, and show me how it's done."

I obeyed, the taste of her now familiar.

Dawn was approaching when the three of us finally collapsed in a heap on my bed. A smile slid across my face as I realized how happy I was. Deep in my gut, I knew I had to quit the shit, get off the glue. All of us did. It struck me like a slap in the face how I had contributed to Kris's marriage crumbling, her drug use, Matt's drug use, my own demise. I'd always prided myself on my excellent attendance, but recently, I'd been written up for missing too many days at work. This job was more than a way for me to get my fix—it had career potential, a corporate ladder to climb, insurance, a 401(k). Wasn't a career what I was looking for?

I remembered a fight between me and my ex-husband, how he had belittled me and mocked me when I told him I wanted to go to college. "To do what?" he had said with a laugh. "You're borderline retarded." That image had spurred me to get my shit together. *I'll prove it to him and the whole world I'm not stupid and I'm not worthless.* Once this shit was gone, I was done for good. The declaration seemed hollow even to me.

CHAPTER 13

I did my last line at work the night before Mari and I flew to California to get more. We were meeting at 5:10 a.m. to catch the earliest flight out, and I'd purposefully stayed up after my shift so that my body would be ready for sleep on the plane. I was out before the plane took off.

When we got to Mari's car in San Jose, she immediately found the little stash in the center console, and we snorted the tiny lines before leaving the airport parking lot.

"Think I'll skip out on the booze," I mentioned casually when we stopped to buy some orange juice at the convenience store. Kris owed me eighty dollars but had only paid me half of it before we'd left. Matt had never contributed anything for the lines he and his friends did. Mari and Patch had stopped paying my way. It had become necessary to conserve what little money I had.

"Well, I can't do the farm stop without it," Mari said.

My mind spun with the memory of the immigrant farmworker. My stomach squeezed, and for a moment, I thought I was going to puke. "You've got a point." I added a small bottle of vodka to our items.

By the time we reached the farm, I felt like a damp, dirty dishcloth. The line we'd done had only been enough to make me feel awake but not high. We slammed our vodka and orange juice, and I felt tipsy more than anything.

"Let's do this thing." Mari looked like a trooper, ready for battle.

I could see the farmworker's smile crackle alive, his pace light and eager, as he skipped toward us when we got out of the car. He threw his arms around our shoulders, and as we walked toward the building, he and Mari conversed back and forth in Spanish, but Mari's tone indicated she had no patience for him this morning.

Once inside, Mari pulled her shirt over her head and held out her arms as if she was about to grab him in a bear hug. "Let's get this shit over with," she mumbled.

Without warning, the man slapped her across the face with an open hand.

"What the fuck!" she yelped as blood poured from her nose. She lurched forward, pushing at his chest, but he grabbed her hair in response, twisting her body away from his, and violently shoved her against the wall. I heard Mari grunt as the breath in her lungs left her body, and I watched as the farmer threw the baggie on the ground at her feet. When he turned toward me, my knees went weak, but thankfully, he stomped out, barking out something in Spanish as he left.

"Let's go," Mari ordered as she bent down and picked up the rock of meth. I followed her back to the car in silence. Her shirt was splattered with blood, but her nose seemed to have stopped flowing. As she stomped on the gas, she tossed the baggie in my lap. "Do me up a big one."

"What happened back there?" I asked, fumbling with the CD and powder.

"He got his fuckin' panties in a knot!" she seethed as I turned my attention to lining us out two big lines. "By the way, if you want to split that with me, I'm going to have to charge you."

I shrugged because, well, what was I supposed to say? As soon as I finished rolling a bill, I offered her the CD case. She leaned over, huffed the substance while driving, and handed the bill back to me.

"Who does that cocksucker think he is?" she asked.

"Well, what'd he say?"

"He knows more English than he pretends," she informed me, "but basically, he was pissed about my 'let's get this over with' comment. As if I enjoy being groped by him! He thinks that I fucking *like* that shit! Like I'm all into it and apparently should be grateful for his sorry ass!" I didn't say anything. Her sideways glance bore into me. "What?"

I hesitated. "Well … as opposed to the alternative?" She said nothing but gave me another hard stare. "Paying for it …" I paused. "With money? There's always that." I deliberately diverted my attention to the passenger-side window. "We have jobs."

"Fuck off." Her tone wasn't angry as much as it was irritated. "You don't know shit. Now grab me another shirt from my bag." I reached back and extracted a tank top from her backpack. She changed shirts while she drove in silence.

When we got to Mike and Patch's place, no one met us in the driveway. Nonetheless, Mari exited the car with flamboyance, slamming the door behind her and swinging her bag with flair. But before she reached the front door, it swung open, and Mike took her in his arms and kissed her fervently. "Hi, baby," he crooned and then looked up to me. "So you're the third wheel this weekend," Mike informed me as I straddled one of the bar stools in the breakfast nook.

"No Patch?"

"Nope. He's gettin' his rocks off with a new play toy this weekend." I arched one eyebrow at him. "Guess she's from the gym or something," he added. "No offense, Dee. We all know you two aren't exclusive, so don't take it personal. You're fucking other people, and he's fucking other people. Everyone is getting laid; everybody's happy." He smiled at me and then turned to Mari. "Well, except me, of course." Mari's face knit into a scowl, causing his face to drop. "I mean, I'm getting laid with you, babe, but no one else. I'm happy! Shit. That came out all wrong," he stammered. The look he gave her rivaled any puppy dog's as she let out a long sigh.

"Fuck it." She took a long drink from her glass. "Let's party."

Our weekend turned out chill. Since I didn't want to trespass in Patch's personal space, I made a bunk in the living room. No television, just a nice bay window with a boring view. There were no curtains, so even at three in the morning, I could watch the country cats and stray dogs slink from shadow to shadow. I doodled, wrote poems, and colored in a coloring book Mari had bought. Overall, it was nice to hang out with no Patch.

In reality, it was a relief to not have to worry about the triple-X sex scene every other hour.

"We can still make this work," Mari explained as I watched her crush the meth with a pestle and mortar as she added additional powder. "You can move some for me, can't you?" I nodded. "Here, try this." She held out a little pile of the powder on a tiny spoon. "What do you think?" It didn't burn my nose as much, nor did I get the intense rush I was craving.

"It's okay."

"Well, I'll split whatever you can get for it, okay? Just don't rip me off, please and thank you." She did a bump from the spoon.

"Rip you off? How is that even possible? You got it for—"

"Stop!" she commanded. "That's not the point. It doesn't matter what I got it for; we're gonna split whatever you sell it for. And try not to do it all," she added. "That's the trick, Dee. Don't do it all." Her green eyes pierced mine. "Seriously, control yourself."

Well, if that wasn't the pot calling the kettle black.

CHAPTER 14

When I got back from California, my answering machine was full. Christopher's messages were sweet and romantic and made me wonder why I was messing around with schizophrenics like Matt and he-hoes like Patch.

Kris's first message was nothing more than a "call me" message, but in the second one, she was in hysterics. I struggled to understand what she was saying through the sobs.

"Hey, I'm home," I said when she answered.

"He's gone."

"Who?" I asked, before realizing.

"Dave. He flipped his shit the night before last."

"Why?" I didn't really care, but it seemed like the right question to ask.

"Told him I didn't think we should be sleeping with you anymore, you know?" I could hear her loyalty to me seep through the phone. "He's getting obsessed with you and the whole sex thing. It's like he's a sex addict or something. You're not mad, are you?"

Confusion settled on me. "Mad about what?"

"That I don't want us all sleeping together anymore."

"It's your marriage, your life. Good grief, it's none of my business." Mad? Relieved was more like it, but there was no need to go there. I soothed her, saying, "To be honest, I didn't really care for him. I think you could do better."

"Threw a chair through the fucking kitchen window." Her voice cracked. "It's boarded up now. Gonna be a fortune to replace."

"That sucks," I continued to console, and listened to her cry until she finally spoke again.

"Did you get any more of that shit?" Guilt stabbed me as I realized she was hooked—addicted—and it was my fault. I had become the bad guy in my own life.

When I talked to Matt, he was normal, no signs of aggression or jealousy. He said he'd missed me and he wanted to see me when I got off work, code for "Let's have sex." I didn't bother calling Christopher back; I'd see him at the club the next night.

At work, Joy stopped me in the hall and asked my permission to touch my crystal necklace. Despite her weirdness, I agreed.

She closed her eyes when she touched it, looking as if she was deep in prayer. When she opened her eyes again, she said, "Please, make an appointment to come to my office. There's so much negativity that needs to be released. The energy you're picking up from your friends is making it gray. Gray is no good when it comes to energy."

"I bet not," I agreed, pushing by her to get to my station to clock in on time.

My shift was a normal everyday shift. Once home, I almost expected to see Matt naked in my bed when I flipped on the light, and he didn't disappoint. He smiled and threw the covers back, exposing his naked hard-on. I stripped as I walked toward him. As we were having sex, he whispered in my ear, "You're not fucking anyone else, are you?"

When I didn't answer, he gave my hair a sharp tug, forcing me to look at him. "Dude, we're not exclusive!" I yelled, but he pulled harder, moving his face close to mine. "But I didn't fuck anyone while I was gone," I said honestly.

"We may not be exclusive, but I tell you who to fuck—got that?" His voice was deep and menacing. Our eyes met. I didn't give a yes or no; this side of Matt I could do without.

When we were lying in bed smoking a bowl, he asked, "Got any of that shit?" I obediently got my wallet and chopped us both a line.

"You still owe me for the last stuff," I reminded him.

"Didn't know you were charging me."

"Well, it's got to get paid for somehow, and yes, I did tell you. Five hundred? That doesn't ring a bell?"

He huffed the line in one breath and then stopped. "Whoa, where's the good stuff?" I looked at him, confused. "This is shit!" he complained. "Not the good shit you usually have. What happened?"

"I have no idea what you're talking about," I replied as I snorted my line. It did taste different.

"Tell your dude I can taste he's cutting it. Don't let him play you for a chump." He looked hard at me and recognized the confusion. "Okay, it means when your dealer stomps on your shit, he cuts up shit like baby laxative or Sudafed." He could see I was still confused. "It's drug math," he said. "Easy stuff. Say you've got an ounce, twenty-four grams. You can divide that by eight and take one eighth for yourself and then replace it with something else. That way, you're getting yours for free. It's common practice, but I'm not putting up with it. This is shitty shit."

My brows knit together, and it was as if he could see into my brain. "It's Kris," he deadpanned.

"Huh?" My head snapped up, and I stared at him. "No, it's not."

"What's your work buddy's name? Mari? It's Mari then. Your dude's not a dude; it's a chick. She looks like a tweaker, anyway. Seriously, I'm not paying for that garbage. If she has a problem with it, have her come to me." He bent down and did another huge line of the drugs he wasn't going to pay for.

"Well, you need to pay me for what you owe at least," I insisted as the phone rang, startling us both.

"I'm coming over," Kris told me when I answered. "Laura's at my parents' house, and Dave keeps calling and calling, and when I answer, he threatens me."

"Unplug the phone."

"I'm coming over."

"Door's open." She disconnected, and in eight minutes, she arrived. When she walked in and saw Matt, she looked at me with wide eyes. "You didn't tell me you had company."

"You didn't give me a chance," I replied and handed the rolled dollar bill to her so she could do the line on the dresser.

"I think I'm going to have to get a restraining order," she said as she huffed the powder, but then Matt grabbed her and kissed her so hard she dropped her purse.

I chopped another three small lines, snorted mine, and offered the rolled dollar bill to them. Matt grabbed the bill and huffed his line and passed the makeshift straw to Kris. She bent over to do her line, and as she did, Matt grabbed her hips and pressed his erection into her ass. His eyes were dancing, his pupils huge. He looked demonic.

"I should probably get going," she informed him as she looked at his fully erect penis. But again, Matt grabbed her, pressed his mouth onto hers, and fumbled with the button on her jeans. She started to pull away, but he grabbed her and shoved her onto the bed. "Or not," she yelped. Her eyes went wide as he reached his hand to the back of her head and moved his penis into her mouth.

I pulled my dress over my head and stood there in my thong panties. Her and my eyes met, and she shrugged her shoulders and pulled off her jeans.

The next morning, Matt was spooning behind me, his hand resting lightly over my breasts. Kris's arm was stretched across his body, her fingers interlaced with his. As stealthily as I could, I slipped out of bed and into the shower. When

I returned, Matt was on top of Kris, the distinct motion of sex occurring below the covers.

"Come join us, baby," Matt said, moving off Kris. She sat up eagerly, and when I approached the bed, she grabbed my hips and plunged her face into my clean, wet pussy. Matt was still hard and started to mount her from behind. She moaned, and I felt close to climax already. Matt's and my eyes met across Kris's back.

"I love you," he mouthed as he fucked my best friend and she sucked and fingered me to orgasm.

CHAPTER 15

After work the next day, Suzy stopped me on the stairs, asking, "Did Kris spend the night last night?"

"Um, yeah … she had too much to drink … didn't want to get a DUI."

"And Matt?"

"Um," I stalled. I hadn't expected this confrontation and couldn't think of a lie fast enough.

"Wow" was all she said, but I wasn't certain if she meant *Wow, that's cool* or *Wow, very uncool* and she felt a bit disgusted. "I'm not telling you how to live your life or preaching morals, but—"

I interrupted her. "Don't do this."

"Me!" she screamed. "Are you kidding me?" I started walking away. "Why won't you let someone care enough about you to worry about you?" she yelled at my back.

As she said it, it reminded me of how Joy had cornered me at work earlier in the day, informing me that she was worried about the company I'd been keeping, explaining again that the amethyst necklace was turning colors because it was attracting and holding negative energy. Trying to convince myself I didn't believe in that kind of stuff, I told her that the necklace was fine, but I found myself holding it to the light on my drive home to see if I noticed a difference. It did appear lighter, but perhaps it was just the power of suggestion.

I held Suzy's stare another few seconds before she asked another question. "You gonna pay rent this month?"

"Holy shit, I forgot!" My mind whirled. What day was it? "Give me a minute!"

I dashed upstairs and grabbed the fifty-dollar bill I'd made Matt leave me when he took a huge helping of the chopped-up powder. Then I dug through my pockets and came up with another forty dollars, plus the forty Kris had finally paid me that I'd left in my purse. That was all the cash I had, and I was still short for rent.

I went back downstairs and gave her the bills. "I'm a bit short this month, but I'll have it to you on payday, okay?"

"Is this money okay to send to school with the kids for lunch money?" Suzy held the money up to the light, closely examining the bills.

"Sure. Why wouldn't it be?" I could see a bit of resin on a bill from using it as a straw.

Her eyes narrowed as she looked at me. "Pot's one thing, but ..." she said, her voice trailing off.

"I don't know what you're talking about." I turned to go back up to my room. "I'm going to the club tonight. Want to join me?"

"It's Tuesday." I looked back over my shoulder at her and shrugged as she continued. "And question. If you have money for the club, why are you short on rent?"

I let out a deep, loud chuckle. "I don't spend my own money at the club. Girl, please!"

She gasped. "Dacia, don't sass me! Have some respect, for cryin' out loud."

"Don't tell me what to do." From the corner of my eye, I saw movement; her kids were watching this confrontation. "Go to bed," I hollered.

"Don't tell me what to do." Suzy's daughter mocked me as we heard running down the hall.

Suzy let out a deep breath. "I don't want to have to evict you, Dee. Please, though, for the kids, try to set a decent example."

I found Christopher in his normal end-of-the-bar spot. He saw me, toasting the air when I came in. It felt like months had passed since I'd seen him, instead of mere days.

"Hey, stranger," I said, plopping onto the stool beside him. He motioned for Doc, and a drink appeared in front of me within a minute.

"When are we going out?" he asked, staring at the dance floor.

"I'm available this weekend." I took a long swallow of my beverage.

"Saturday?"

"Um ..." I mentally checked my schedule. "I can trade my shift with someone that day so I'll be working until six; that would be the earliest I could get out of there."

"I'll pick you up at seven then," he said.

"Pick me up?" I laughed, taking another sip of my drink.

"Um, yeah. It's a date. Haven't you ever been on a date before?" I thought of all the company dinners Leonard had taken me to when I felt like nothing more than an accessory on his arm. Then my mind wandered further back, to high school, prom, group date nights, and then those nights I had snuck out through my window and gone to the bars with a fake ID.

"Of course, I have," I said with confidence.

"Then you should know that the first rule of a date is that the guy—in this case, me—picks up the girl—in this case, you. It's protocol."

I couldn't help but smile. "Okay, seven on Saturday."

Just then, the music picked up. I never waited until a dude asked me to dance. I just hit the floor and went with whatever I was feeling. Grabbing my drink, I moved toward the dance floor. My white-girl moves usually made me somewhat of a spectacle, but I didn't mind. In fact, I secretly liked it when everyone watched me.

When the last-call announcement came, I thanked Christopher, who had bought three of my five drinks. With complete rationale, I explained to him my theory about leaving early and avoiding the cops.

"I'll walk you out," he offered and hopped off the stool and placed his hand on the small of my back as he threaded me through the waning crowd.

"You want to come to my place and smoke a bowl?" he asked when we got out into the night air. I glanced into the bushes where Matt and I had been just a few weeks before.

"If I come home and fuck you tonight, there will be no reason to take me out Saturday, now will there?" I said as I unlocked my car.

I noticed Christopher's eyes slide up and down my body as I slid into the driver's seat. He stood in the open door and leaned in as I put the key in the ignition.

"I never said anything about fucking." His voice was sweet and innocent.

I smiled and looked up at him, and then my heart dropped into my gut. From the corner of my eye, I saw Matt in his car across the parking lot, waving and pointing enthusiastically to a handsome man sitting in his passenger seat. I didn't want Christopher to see them, so I held his gaze.

"You don't know me very well, do you?" A smile slid across my face as my eyes went wide and innocent. Christopher bent into the car as if he was going to kiss me, so I turned my face, allowing him to peck my cheek.

"See you Saturday," he said, barely concealing the disappointment of his misguided lips. Once he was back inside, I got back out of my car and acknowledged Matt.

"Get in the back, fucker," he said to the man. "Get in, get in," he said urgently to me. I obeyed, and Matt sped from the parking lot. He went west and got on the freeway.

"What's up?" I asked, looking from him to the handsome man in the back seat.

"We're going back to your house."

"Why'd we go this way?"

"I want you to be ready when we get there."

"Ready for what?"

He reached across me and released the seat so I flopped backward. His hand shot up my skirt and into my panties. "Taste this," he said to the man in the back, offering him his finger. Sensually, he sucked my scent off Matt's finger. "Get you some," Matt said and roughly pushed my shirt up, exposing my breasts. The man in the back yanked the shirt over my head and took one of my boobs in his mouth, then stretched his arms in between my legs and started to rub me.

"After our great night with your best friend the other night, I wanted to return the favor. We're going to take you on a ride you'll never forget."

When he pulled in front of my house, I asked for my shirt back. "I threw it out the window," Matt answered.

"No, you didn't."

"Yeah, I did. In fact, you're going to walk in topless and hope we don't run into that hot little roomie of yours." His smile was wicked. "If we do, it'll be an orgy instead of a threesome." He winked and got out. "Come on now; don't be shy. If I had a dog collar and leash, I'd put them on Steve-o here and have you two parade in topless together."

Steve smiled like a kid in a candy store as I glanced at the dash clock—2:38 a.m. Realistically, no one should be up. I quickly got out of the car, one arm across my breasts, and jogged to the dark porch.

"Such a shame the light isn't on," Matt whispered as I fumbled with the key.

"Be quiet. I don't want to wake Suzy." We snuck up the stairs and went to my room. I grabbed my robe.

"Nope," Matt said, taking it from me. "In fact, take your skirt off. I want Steve to see you naked." I undid the skirt, and it fell to the floor. "Bend over."

"What?"

"Just do it!" He grabbed my hair and tugged my head forward until I bent over. "You're gonna fuck that pussy good and hard, you hear me?" Matt instructed Steve. I stood back up and turned to them.

"Let's do a line first," I offered. I was ready for another one. Within minutes, we were so high the men had taken off their clothes and were both as hard as rocks.

"Wow, Matt. Did you interview your friends to find the one with the biggest cock?" I asked, admiring Steve's penis.

"Damn, that *is* big," he agreed. "When we're both fucking you, I'll take your ass, okay?" He grabbed my hair again and pinned my arms above my head. "Help yourself," he said to Steve.

At that, Steve immediately knelt in front of me and got to work, licking and sucking between my legs. His fingers went inside me, and I moaned with pleasure as Matt grabbed me around my waist, lifting me up and down so Steve's hand went farther and farther inside me. I came all over Steve's face and hand. "Good girl," Matt cooed in my ear. "Are you ready?"

"Not yet," I said with a coy smile. "You said you were returning the favor by bringing this fine male specimen to me, didn't you?"

"Fuck yeah, I did," he said as he kissed my neck. "A woman like you needs more than one cock to satisfy her."

"Maybe," I considered. "You know what? I want you to suck Steve." I stepped out of his embrace and met his eye.

"No way. Isn't going to happen." Matt glanced at Steve, who smiled his goofy grin.

"Sure it is." The grin across my face rivaled that of the Cheshire cat from *Alice in Wonderland*. "If you ever want to see me go down on another woman, you're going to do this for me," I instructed, feeling bold. "Show me how it's done, Matt. I did it for you with my best friend. Now it's your turn."

"That does seem fair," Steve interjected.

"No one asked you," Matt snapped. A long moment passed. I knelt and took Steve in my mouth. He moaned.

"See, easy." I looked at Matt. "Come on. I have a feeling Steve won't mind." I motioned for Matt to kneel next to me. To my surprise, he did. "There you go," I said as I moved Steve into Matt's mouth. Steve moaned so hard I thought he would orgasm right then. "You want to try too, Steve?" He nodded, his look a combination of pleasure and pain. I positioned them in a sixty-nine, their mouths full of each other's penises. Steve's eyes were closed, a look of ecstasy on his face. Matt's eyes were open, concentrating on doing it right.

Our eyes met, and I rocked back on my knees. I couldn't help but revel in the power I felt in that moment. It turned me on. I had convinced two heterosexual men that giving each other a blow job was just the thing to do. I giggled to myself. This was fun.

CHAPTER 16

Matt snored softly behind me, his arms draped over my waist. With a pillow under his head and a towel for a blanket, Steve slept on the floor. Stepping over him carefully, I slipped into the bathroom and brushed my teeth.

When I returned, Steve was awake and asked to use the restroom. I pointed him in the right direction, and as soon as he left, Matt motioned for me to join him in the bed. Once we were cuddled together, my body relaxed into his as I reveled in the thought of our amazing night. Suddenly, he grabbed my hair and jerked my head to face him.

"That pussy is mine," he hissed in my ear. "You don't fuck no one unless I say so. You got it? And another thing." He looked around, afraid someone else could hear what he was about to say. "What happened last night never happened. You got that? You never, ever breathe a word of what we did last night." He pulled my hair harder to make a point, a hint of violence dancing in his eyes. "And one *more* thing." His eyes narrowed as I shuddered. "I saw that fuckin' pip-squeak walkin' you to your car last night." His tone sounded serious. "You're not fucking him. You got that? No. No. No."

At that moment, Steve walked back in, causing the heavy mood to change in an instant. He was all smiles and cheerful. "We should do that again, you guys. I enjoyed every minute."

"Um, I don't think so, dude," Matt said, an edge to his voice. "In fact, I was just telling Dacia here that what happened last night never leaves this room. We clear on that, buddy?" Steve shrugged and nodded.

"My car!" I said in alarm. "We gotta go get it!" I jumped up and started to dress.

As we emerged from my room ten minutes later, Suzy stood at the bottom of the stairs in her robe and matching slippers, drinking a cup of coffee. She smiled at me initially, but when she saw Matt, her face dropped, and when she saw Steve, anger filled her eyes.

"Good morning," each of us said in turn as we passed her, walking out the door.

Once I had my car, I went home and got back in bed. I had four and a half hours before I had to be to work, and I'd barely had two and a half hours of sleep. With the shades drawn and the phone turned off, I was ready to get some shut-eye when I heard a light tapping at my door.

"Everything okay in there?" Suzy let herself in and surveyed the darkness.

"Yup, just gonna take a nap before my shift."

"Drink too much again last night?" I let the words float between us as if I hadn't heard them. "Did both of those guys stay here last night?"

"Suzy, I need to get some sleep."

"It's none of my business, I know, but Dacia …" Her words trailed off, and I was thankful the dimness of the room hid her expression. "I don't want my kids to see this kind of thing, you know?"

"Of course! I'm pretty sure neither one of your kids knew those guys were here."

"That's not exactly my point."

"Isn't it?" My tone was a bit sharper than I'd expected, but I just wanted to go to sleep. My body ached pleasantly from the night before; two men at the same time was quite fun. Exhaustion slithered through me as I thought about the boy-on-boy sixty-nine, but despite being tired, my body shuddered with power anyway. Again, I was grateful for the dark.

"Well …" Suzy began, but instead of finishing her thought, she backed out of the room, and I fell into a deep sleep within minutes.

When my alarm went off, it jolted me from a deep sleep—I momentarily forgot where I was. As soon as I got my bearings, I raced through my shower and got ready for work.

When I returned to my room, I noticed the flashing light on the answering machine; it indicated I had three new messages. As I pushed play, I realized I hadn't noticed them the night before.

The first message was Kris simply asking me to call. I listened to it twice in an effort to decipher her mood, but I couldn't. The next two were from Christopher. In the first message, his voice was laced with concern, asking if I was all right. Why wouldn't I be all right? I wondered. But I quickly understood.

In his second message, his urgency bordered on tears as he spoke. "Where are you, Dacia? Your car is still in the parking lot at the bar! I called the police, and they said you're not in the drunk tank. What happened after I walked you out? Please call me. If I don't hear from you, I'm going to report you missing. Please. Let me know you're okay. I'm worried about you."

I stared in disbelief at the machine. How long had it been since someone had worried about me? First Joy, then Suzy, and now Christopher. People cared about me. Then I sabotaged those thoughts and wondered if I should consider his concern sweet or stalkerish. As I listened to the message again, I leaned toward thinking it was sweet.

I checked the clock again—it was noon, so he'd be at work. I called him back at his house and left a vague yet reassuring message that I had, in fact, arrived home safely and thanked him for the concern. For good measure, I added that I was looking forward to our date. Then I dialed Kris.

"He served me divorce papers." Her voice cracked.

"Aw, c'mon, that's not entirely a bad thing!" I reassured her.

"Yeah, it is. I can't afford this place on my own," she cried. "I talked to my supervisors at work and put in for a transfer to Ogden. It's closer to my mom and dad, and they can help me with the baby." Selfishly, I considered how inconvenient this was on my end. Not only was she moving away, but I'd have to drive an hour to get my weed.

At work, I ran into Joy before I even clocked in, her eyes filled with motherly concern. "Dacia! Didn't I tell you to take off that necklace?" she reprimanded as she placed her hand an inch above my throat. "There are negative energies attached to this stone … spirits." With irritation, I tried to walk past her, but she kept going. "Dark spirits are attached to your aura too. You really need to come into my office so we can cleanse your—"

"Joy, stop!" I exhaled slowly. "Just stop." I pushed my way past her and settled in for my shift.

Mari came in at her scheduled time, but I immediately noticed her eyes were redder than usual. It looked like she'd been crying, but she didn't say anything as she clocked in and took her calls as usual. I passed her a note to ask if she was all right.

When she passed it back, it read, *Mikey and I are through.* I stood and looked over the divider at the tears rolling down her face. She looked miserable.

CHAPTER 17

The night of my date with Christopher, I wondered what I was so nervous about—I didn't want a relationship with him! I had only agreed to go out with him so that he'd get it out of his system and quit asking me out. But then I considered the fact that I hadn't been on a *real* date in years—perhaps that was the reason for my nerves.

When I had given Christopher my address two nights before at the club, he had stuffed the piece of paper into his shirt pocket, offering me no details on the evening. And since I didn't know what we were doing, I couldn't decide what to wear. I settled on jeans and a fancy top with boots. That way, I could look dressed up or casual, depending on what we did.

He arrived right on time, pulling up in his '72 Chevy that he'd had restored. It was immaculately clean, painted in two-tone red and white, the chrome gleaming in the setting sun. Christopher got out of the truck, revealing his date-night outfit—jeans and a button-down denim shirt. It looked a bit like a uniform.

"Where we headed?" I asked as he helped me into the truck.

He shrugged, a glint in his eye. "There's a doobie for you in the ashtray."

I sparked it up while he walked around to his side, hopped in, and started the engine. We drove north, into the city. I was surprised when he took the City Creek exit and began driving up the canyon. I had expected him to take the main downtown off-ramp.

"Where are you taking me?" I asked as we moved away from the city lights.

"Just wait," he answered, a smirk playing at the corner of his mouth.

We wound up in the canyon, and he pulled into a camp area. I watched in wonder as the trees' shadows danced in the light of the full moon that was cresting on the horizon.

"Wait here. I'll be right back." He got out and went to the back of the truck. As I gazed at the rising moon, I thought about the last time it had been full. It was the first time I'd been in Salinas, when I'd met Mikey and Patch. It had been only a month. My life had slipped and changed in only one moon cycle in ways I couldn't have expected. As I continued to stare at the reflecting orb, I thought of Mari's breakup. I hoped she would figure it out so we could continue getting our shit. *No,* I argued with myself, *I'm quitting, done with it. Her relationship doesn't have a bearing on my life or my happiness.*

Totally lost in thought, I jumped in surprise when Christopher opened the passenger door. "Ready."

As I got out, my mouth dropped open as I stared at what looked like something straight out of a Hollywood movie set. A table set with dinnerware and candles and surrounded by two chairs stood before me. Christopher pulled out one of the chairs and gestured for me to sit down.

I continued to gawk at the chilled bottle of wine that sat next to a beautiful tray arranged with several types of cheese and an abundance of fruit. Then, before I could utter a word, hundreds of twinkling lights lit up all around me as "Thank God for You" by Sawyer Brown began to play from the speakers in the truck. Christopher appeared from the shadows and gently placed a plate of food in front of me. Then he disappeared. I studied what was on the plate: a croissant stuffed with chicken salad, purple grapes, and two little triangles of white cheese. I took in the view of the city and the sparkling lights, and my heart swelled with the music—it was all so enchanting. Christopher returned with his own plate and sat down across from me.

"Eat," he said, a huge smile breaking across his face.

"This … this is beautiful," I said with appreciation.

"Not as beautiful as you," he answered, toasting his wineglass in my direction.

"That was a bit corny, but sweet." I grinned and took a bite of food. It was delicious.

"That's me, corny but sweet."

We continued to eat, the conversation natural. Once dinner was over, he turned off the sparkly white lights, and we lounged in the bed of the truck, watching the moon and stars while smoking the rest of the joint.

"See that star?" he said and pointed up to the north. "That's the star Algol, the eye of Medusa."

"Medusa?" I asked and handed him back the joint, recalling the taunting of my classmates.

"Yeah. Do you know your Greek mythology?"

"No, just that she was ugly." I forced a laugh; it sounded hard and not natural.

"Actually, she was the most beautiful woman in all the land."

"Really?" I said, looking back at the star.

"Yeah, she's got a bad rap. Athena was jealous of her beauty and turned her hair to snakes." He put his arm around me. "I love that kind of stuff," he said.

"The kids at school used to call me Medusa," I admitted.

"Because they were jealous of your beauty, I bet." He smiled at me, and I felt my heart soften. I still wasn't physically attracted to him, but the night had gone so well I let him keep his hand on the back of my neck.

"I had a great time tonight," I offered.

"The night's not over," he said as he leaned in and kissed me.

CHAPTER 18

Kris found an apartment in Ogden, about an hour away. She assumed I would come help her pack and move before work on a Saturday. It annoyed me a bit, but I did it anyway. She was my oldest friend, after all, and I knew there would be Bloody Marys and pot. We chatted while we boxed up her kitchen, and I told her all about my official date with Christopher.

"So, you just fucked him right there in the back of the truck?" she asked. I nodded and continued to wrap newspaper around dinner plates. "And it was good?"

"Really good. Maybe the best ever."

She cocked one eyebrow at me. "What about Matt?"

"I don't know what to do with him." Feeling her gaze, I kept my eyes on my task. "He told me he'd freak if I went out with Christopher."

"Yet he fucks your best friend and enjoys watching you fuck his best friend—or should I say *friends*." I gave her a dirty look. "He's trouble, Dacia. Seriously, run; don't walk. Get away from him."

I knew she was right, but I had enjoyed our naughty escapades. Besides, there was no way he would find out about Christopher. The thought of Christopher made my insides warm. Lovemaking with him was just that—it wasn't fuckin' or nasty or wham-bam-thank-you-ma'am. It had been sweet, soft, and enjoyable. My needs came first. I couldn't even count the number of orgasms I'd had. He was possibly the best lover I'd ever been with. My ears began to burn at the thought of his mouth on me, and remembering the way he'd gone down on me made my toes curl.

"You're thinking about him," Kris teased.

"Who?" I asked, smacked out of my daydream by her words.

"You know." She smiled, took the pile of paper-wrapped plates I'd been working on, and secured them in a heavy cardboard box. "I can see it in your eyes. You're gonna fall for the one guy you told me you'd never hook up with."

"I don't know …"

"Wanna bet?" Her grin had taken over her entire face, although she tried to suppress it.

"Dude, I'm not interested."

"Then why did you sleep with him?"

"It was convenient?"

"Liar." She pushed back. "Are you going out with him again?"

"Actually, yes. We have a date on Friday." She gave me that I-told-you-so look. "To be fair, though, I'm going out with Matt and Steve on Thursday."

"That's my idea of a double date." Kris smirked. "What about the California guy?"

"Not sure." I started wrapping the ceramic cereal bowls. "Mari said her and Mikey split up, so I don't know."

"Well, I hope they work things out," she said, and I gave her a puzzled look. "What? That's where you get the shit, right?"

"Not exactly. I mean yes, but not really."

"Oh well then. Who cares if they're over, right?" She laughed and continued to load the moving boxes.

At work, I had started stalking Joy's schedule in an attempt to avoid her. Each time she saw me, she felt the need to tell me that dark entities were still attached to my aura and it was more and more urgent that I get them cleared away. For the most part, I thought she was full of shit. That being said, I had to admit my physical appearance had changed.

Because of the drugs, my weight had dipped twenty pounds, to the point where my clothes didn't fit and my face looked gaunt. Now, I'm tall. Like I said before, I come from Viking stock—at least that's what my grandfather had always told me. I wasn't "little," to say the least, so twenty pounds wasn't a huge issue, but in addition to the clothes and my face, my skin had taken on an ashen color. I wanted to blame my skin tone on the winter weather and the fact I wasn't getting any sun, but I knew I was in denial because there were other signs too. My hair was limp and brittle. The muscles in my legs and arms seemed weak, and I wasn't as active. What I couldn't admit was that the drugs were breaking down my body and that I looked like a Scandinavian refugee who hadn't eaten in months.

On my Thursday-night date with Matt and Steve, we decided to go to a club called High Wired to see the band Mötley Crüe. I was so excited since I'd loved this band for as long as I could remember.

Because it was a smaller venue, we were able to get close to the stage. It was nice to be in between the two men. It kept the crowd from pitching me around. I held the crystal around my neck and pictured myself having a threesome with Nikki Sixx and Tommy Lee.

Toward the end of the last set, Nikki Sixx pointed into the crowd at me. He did the "come here" thing with his index finger, just like he did in the "Looks That Kill" video. I'd watched that video dozens of times on MTV. My heart raced as I was lifted off the ground by a set of hands. In the craziness, Matt had helped me get on Steve's shoulders. Nikki reached over the first two rows of people and planted his lips on my mouth. I jammed my tongue into his and threaded my fingers into his long, sticky black hair. With one hand, he reached around my head, and we made out as the crowd went wild.

Steve's head bobbed around with my added weight on his shoulders, and I pictured Matt steadying him. When the long kiss was over, I was so breathless and excited that I was practically on the verge of an orgasm. Without thinking, I opened my shirt and exposed my bare breasts toward the stage. Nikki reached out, twisted one of my nipples as he laughed, and then walked back to the center of the stage to continue the set. When they were done, the lights went out, and the crowd went wild, screaming for an encore.

Matt helped me off Steve's shoulders. "Let's beat the crowd and dip out now!" he shouted so both Steve and I could hear.

"It's cool. I think I'll stay here," I shouted back.

"Not on your life," Matt said, a sharklike smile taking over his face. He roughly grabbed my arm. "You've had enough."

I gave him a dirty look as he steered me toward the exit, but once we were outside, I jerked away from his hold. "You're not my dad, motherfucker," I said as I walked in front of him, anger swelling in my chest.

"We're on a date," Matt insisted, hurrying to catch up with me. "A lady doesn't go off to gangbang the band while on a date with her main squeeze."

"Fuck off, Matt." Between the drugs we'd done earlier and the mass amounts of alcohol in my system, I felt brazen, strong. Matt grabbed my arm and twisted my body to face him.

"Remember—I tell you who to fuck!" His eyes went wild. "And it sure as hell isn't going to be a rock-and-roll band that won't let me watch or participate and would give you an STD to boot. You're mine. What part of that don't you get?" As I tried to pull away, he grabbed my hair. "Mine!"

"Stop it!" I shouted. Steve had joined us and shouted at Matt to let me go.

Here was my chance. As Matt turned to yell at Steve, I used all my weight to push into him. I caught him off guard, and he stumbled backward, releasing my hair. When I straightened up, my face suddenly jerked to the right as a stinging sensation burned my face. He'd slapped me!

"You motherfucker!" I screamed when the realization of what had happened hit me.

Thankfully, Steve wrapped his arms around my waist and pulled me away from Matt, but at that point, red and blue lights had appeared above the car tops. I winced as two cop cars rounded the parking lot and stopped in front of the three of us. Matt and Steve exchanged worried looks, a flicker of fear in Matt's eyes. One officer got out.

"Everything okay here?" he asked me and then looked to the two men.

"No! This motherfucker just—" I started.

"Yes, Officer. Everything is fine," Steve interjected, taking charge. Matt walked away from us as I touched my face—it had started to swell a bit, and I could feel my eye puffing up.

"Sir," the second officer called to Matt, "step back over by your friends, please."

As Matt ignored the officer and kept walking, the flashing lights from the cop cars turned the parking lot into a dance floor from a nightmare. It made me dizzy and nauseated.

This time, the second officer's voice rose. "Sir, we need you to come back over here."

Without warning, Matt took off in a sprint across the parking lot. The second officer took off after him as the first officer called for backup.

"What the hell is he doing?" I asked Steve, who slowly shook his head as we watched the two officers wrestle Matt to the ground and cinch his hands behind his back with a plastic zip tie.

Now that the concert was over, hundreds of people poured out the front doors of the club. I could hear some of the people as they passed by. "Better them than us, huh? Poor fuckers. Wrong place at the wrong time."

I looked at Steve, his face expressionless, as the first officer walked back up to us and asked for our IDs. I fished mine from my purse as Steve got his from his wallet.

"What's your boyfriend's name?" the officer asked me.

"He's *not* my boyfriend," I hissed.

"So, you're going to press charges then?" I looked at him, confused. "We saw him slap you. That's assault, ma'am."

"Matthew Mabbutt," I blurted out. *Didn't I just tell Kris I wasn't sure what to do with him?* I thought. I guessed I needed a sign, a revelation. This seemed as good as any.

I heard Steve exhale and say, "Shit." When I turned to look at him, he was shaking his head.

CHAPTER 19

Steve and I ended up at Denny's for french fries and brown gravy after the cops let us go. The waitress brought me some ice in a baggie for my face. They had arrested Matt, although I was confused as to why they took him, since I hadn't actually pressed charges. With sad eyes, Steve gently explained to me that I wasn't the only girl in Matt's life, but I felt that still didn't explain why they would have arrested Matt.

"Another woman?"

I could see in his face he didn't want this conversation to continue. "She got pregnant."

"Oh." My attitude changed immediately at the thought of another woman carrying Matt's baby. Was it jealousy I was feeling? Relief? Confusion gripped my throat. I told myself I didn't care, yet here I was, fighting emotion. "Are they getting married?"

Now I was really confused. On the one hand, I hated Matt—he was controlling and manipulative, mean and aggressive. But on the other hand, well … we had really great sex, and when he was sober and straight, he was nice, kind of … a little bit.

"No, uh … she lost the babies, actually—twins." Tears flooded Steve's eyes. He was so sensitive and sweet. How in the world had he got mixed up with Matt? "It was Matt's fault."

"What was Matt's fault?"

"We … um … you know," he said, fighting to control himself, "like at your house the other night, um … but not … we've never done …" His voice trailed off as the image of man-on-man oral sex flooded both our minds. "But we—"

"Yeah, I don't need the details," I interrupted as I twirled one of the fries in the gravy.

"When she told him she was pregnant," he continued, "she was scared, worried. Normal concerns, right?"

I nodded.

"For a moment, I thought maybe I'd got her pregnant. They could have been my children. We hadn't used protection. But ..." He swallowed hard, the shimmer of fresh tears in his eyes. "He beat her." The words were so soft I barely made them out. "With his fists." That I heard. "In the stomach." My own stomach rolled at those words. Now I saw anger flash on Steve's face. "I wasn't there, but I wished I had been. I would have stopped him. He apparently went apeshit crazy. Almost killed her. She called 911 as soon as Matt left. Once the first baby died, they did what they could to save the second one ..."

"Oh my god," I mumbled.

"Yeah, it was bad. Not only did she lose the babies, but she had all sorts of other injuries: a fractured skull, a concussion, internal bleeding, four broken ribs, and a dislocated wrist," he said. My insides clenched as the memory of Matt's viselike grip around my wrist flashed through my mind.

"She pressed charges. There's been a bench warrant for his arrest for months," Steve admitted, his attention shifting back to the food. "You're a good girl, Dacia. You're seriously better off without him."

I nodded, knowing he was right.

We went back to his place, and Steve's soft snoring floated in from the adjacent room as I fell into a fitful sleep on his couch.

Right before dawn, I went into his room and slipped under the covers, his warm body heating mine within seconds. He curled around me as I climbed onto his morning wood. He made noises of protest, but I rocked back and forth until both of us climaxed.

"What just happened does not leave this room," he whispered in my ear as he held me. "I'm being serious, Dacia. Matt can never find out, okay?"

"He's not the boss of me," I said jokingly. "I'll fuck who I want."

"No." Steve's eyes went hard with intensity. "I'll deny it to my death. Did you not understand what I told you last night? You really should stay away from him, Dee. He's dangerous."

The hair on the back of my neck prickled, and I agreed to keep our lovemaking a secret.

It was nearly noon when Steve dropped me off at my house to get ready for work. Suzy met me at the front door.

"I had to unplug your phone." Her words were clipped with annoyance. "It rang off the hook last night, and then this morning, *my* phone started ringing nonstop. It's a recording from the county jail … a *collect call from jail*, Dacia. What's going on?" I feigned innocence and shrugged. "Well, whoever it is, tell them to stop!" she shouted as I climbed the stairs to my room, bobbing my head in a subconscious nod.

Suzy had ripped my phone and answering machine from the wall. When I plugged the answering machine back in, more than a dozen messages waited for me. Only one was from Christopher, reminding me about our date the next night. The rest of them were automated messages from the Salt Lake County Jail asking me to accept a collect call.

Before I could delete the messages, the phone rang, and an automated voice came through the receiver. "Hello. This is a collect call from the Salt Lake County Jail." There was a pause for the inmate to record his name before it continued. "Answer your fucking phone," Matt's angry voice boomed before the recording resumed, "would like to speak to you. Press 1 to accept the charges. Press 2 to disconnect the call." I pressed 1.

"Did you fuck him?" was the first thing out of his mouth when I said hello.

"And good morning to you too."

"Get me the fuck out of here!" he demanded.

"What's going on, Matt? I swear I didn't press charges, so why are they still holding you? Be honest with me." Of course, I knew the answer, but I wanted to see what he'd say. I considered the fact that he might have talked to Steve and Steve might have told him what I knew. But it was also possible that he hadn't spoken to Steve yet. I'd give him a chance to fess up.

"Just a fucked-up misunderstanding." His voice softened slightly. "I need your help, please."

"A misunderstanding?" I said indignantly. "Stop calling here. And don't call Suzy's phone, okay?"

"Listen to me!" he screamed. "Don't hang up!"

"We're done, Matt." I sounded calmer than I felt.

"Don't fuck him, please," he whined.

"We're through. Over. I don't want to hear from you again."

"Please, please, *please* come get me. You're my one and only. You're it for me. Listen … we've got a good thing going. Please. I'm begging. Please get me out of here. I love you, Dacia. I really, really love you."

I hung up.

CHAPTER 20

At work on Friday, the anticipation over knowing I would see Christopher made me giddy, so much so that I chided myself about it. I knew it was a going-nowhere relationship, as in I could never see myself getting involved with him. But that being said, I wasn't actually "dating" any of the other men I was sleeping with. Conveniently, Matt was out of the picture.

Christopher and I were dating, and, of course, sleeping together. I had been thinking of that too—how well he balanced the tender and passionate sides of lovemaking. I made a mental note to grab my carryall bag in case I ended up spending the night. My body ached at the memory of his touch, and I was excited for more.

"Why don't you just admit you're falling for this guy?" Kris asked over the phone.

Looking in the mirror, I held the receiver with my shoulder and scrutinized the makeup I'd applied to my puffy eye where Matt had slapped me. "Because I'm not." The words sounded hollow.

"I think you are," she bantered.

"He's too short for me." Those words sounded trivial.

"Well, now you're just being dumb and superficial."

"Says my five-foot-four friend," I mumbled as I applied lipstick.

"I'm five-six."

"Whatever." I surveyed my face and glanced at the clock. "Gotta run, chica."

"Well, I hope you come to your senses before someone else scoops him up, Dacia. He's a nice guy. What, are you allergic to men that are good to you?"

"Buh-bye," I sung as I hung up.

He arrived on time and, ever the gentleman, walked to the door to get me.

Suzy got there first and invited him in. Her questions reminded me of a parent interviewing his or her child's first date. As restless as I was to go, Christopher seemed to enjoy the extra attention.

After several minutes of casual chitchat, we finally broke away. He drove toward Little Cottonwood Canyon.

"You're looking extra hot tonight," he commented appreciatively.

"Thank you." I smiled, putting my hand on his knee. "You look mighty dapper yourself."

"I know you're into different fantasies and stuff …" His voice trailed off as he avoided my eye, causing my mind to run wild.

"You mean group sex?" I tried to remain playful, but he turned to me in shock. "Well … what about being with two women then?"

"Good god, woman, what man hasn't thought of that? But no, that's not what I had in mind." A long moment of silence between us turned uncomfortable. I watched out the window and waited for him to continue. "So, there's this fancy bar next to the restaurant we're going to …"

"You wanna have sex in the bathroom?" I guessed.

"No! God! Stop!" Even though his words were harsh, I heard my suppressed laughter. "Nothing that complicated. Geez," he said and sighed. "So, I'm short, obviously." This time, I suppressed the laughter, as he held up his hand for me to stay quiet. "Time and time again, I go out and meet nice women. We talk, have a few drinks, you know?" I nodded. "But when it comes closing time, they walk away from me, looking for other dudes that are taller, better-looking, et cetera."

"Bitches," I said, even though I had done this exact thing more than once.

He looked at me and rolled his eyes. "Anyway, what I want you to do, if you're up for it, is go in first, by yourself—"

"Huh?" I didn't understand where this was going.

"No, listen. Go in, flirt, do your thing. Light up the room, and get every man in the bar to ogle at your every move. Have them buy you a few drinks. Laugh, flirt some more, make them think they stand a chance bedding you, okay?"

"Okay …" I agreed hesitantly.

"So then, I'll show up and take a seat at the end of the bar. No one will even know I'm there, but you'll see me. I'll buy you a drink." I could see the wheels turn in his eyes as I watched him work out the scenario. "Eventually, you'll work your way over to where I'm sitting, and we'll act like we don't know each other … if that's okay."

"Sure." This idea was turning me on. I reached my hand between his legs. Gently, he took it and put it back in my lap.

"Later, my dear." He turned and smiled at me as we pulled into the parking lot of the bar. "This works for you?" His eyes danced, his smile reaching every bit of his face.

"Sure," I agreed as I got out. "Easy-peasy. See you in a bit."

I strutted up to the front door of the bar. The bouncer briefly eyed me and then opened the door, and I waltzed in. Christopher had been right; this club was high end.

The patrons, wearing either casual business suits or expensive ski wear, milled around the room as I approached the bar and ordered a Cape Cod. Almost instantly, one of the seated men motioned for the bartender and told him to put my drink on his tab.

"Thank you," I purred, toasting him as I slid onto a bar stool and introduced myself. He was middle aged and outdoorsy-looking and reeked of money—not my type.

A few minutes later, another man sat on the other side of me and offered to buy my next drink. As I finished it, I noticed the club had got crowded. Since I still hadn't seen Christopher, I accepted a third man's invitation to dance, but when we returned to the bar, I noticed Christopher, sitting at the end of the bar with his beer. He raised his glass to me so casually I wouldn't have noticed if I hadn't been looking for some sign he'd seen me.

Another drink appeared as if by magic. When I questioned the bartender where it had come from, he motioned to the end of the bar—to Christopher. I lifted my glass in a salute. The man I had just danced with asked if I wanted to join him and his friends at their table, but I politely declined as the men on either side of me started a friendly banter on who would buy my next drink. Now, knowing Christopher was watching, I laughed and flirted and really turned up the sex appeal.

After each of my bar buddies had bought me another drink, I apologized and said I thought it was time for me to head home. The one on my left asked for my number. I jotted down a fake number on a napkin and bade them all good night. The alcohol buzz had taken a hold of me. I staggered a bit to the end of the bar and took a seat next to Christopher. He motioned for the bartender.

"Water?" he asked. I nodded as he leaned in and whispered, "You are so fucking gorgeous."

"Thank you," I mumbled, his eyes remaining on the men as we leaned our heads together.

"You ready to go eat?" I nodded yes, and as he helped me off the stool and steered me out of the club, the other men's jaws dropped.

"That was amazing," he gushed as the hostess sat us at a candlelit table. "It was perfect. The looks on those dudes' faces when we left? It was priceless. You have no idea how much you made my night."

"You're welcome," I slurred. "Easiest fantasy fulfillment ever."

"I don't want to hear about any others." He laughed as the waitress set a basket of warm bread on the table. I smiled and took a bite of the bread. I needed something to absorb the alcohol. It was thick in my mouth. I took a drink of water and swallowed it down. Who was I kidding? I needed more than a chunk of bread. I excused myself to go to the bathroom.

Digging through my purse, I found a vial with a small amount of meth at the bottom. Using a toothpick, I scraped it out. There was more than I had thought. I snorted it all. Instantly, I felt more awake, more in control. I splashed water on my face and then fixed my makeup and hair. After a few deep breaths, I returned to Christopher.

"Oh shit, did you throw up?"

"No. Do I look bad?" I asked, reflexively raising my hands to my face.

"No, not at all. You just look, uh … more sober."

"It's the bread," I lied as I took another warm bun from the basket, placing it on the plate in front of me. "It absorbed all the alcohol." I was proud of myself for coming up with a believable reason. Then I chided myself for lying. Guilt stabbed at me as I felt the drugs course through my veins. *I'm quitting; I'm done.* It had become a mantra. I tore off a tiny piece of bread and put it in my mouth. Because it was hard to eat when I was this high, I sucked the bread until it turned into a ball of dough in my mouth, and I spit it into a napkin when I pretended to wipe my mouth.

I realized the stuff I'd found in the bottom of my purse hadn't been cut, and even that little amount made me higher than usual. I felt my jaw working from side to side and consciously stopped myself. More guilt tangled my gut. I ordered soup and salad, knowing that would be the easiest food to get down. I noticed Christopher slipped a folded paper to the waitress when she took our order.

"I hope you don't mind, but I took the liberty of getting us a room. We've both had too much to drink to go back down the canyon. I hope that's okay." He reached for my hand and held it gently, his thumb rubbing the back of my knuckles.

"It is." Suddenly, I wished I wasn't high or drunk. In that moment, I allowed the happiness to wash over me. Looking around the fancy restaurant, I took in the aroma of the delicious food and watched my date admire me. If he were a cartoon, there would have been heart shapes fluttering out of his eyes.

I allowed myself to be happy for a moment, pushing the guilt of the drugs to the back of my mind. *I'm quitting; I'm done,* I promised myself again. *I'm not getting more. I'm quitting; I'm done.* Life was beautiful. I had a good job, I had this great guy in my life, and Matt was behind bars—no more of the hard drugs for me.

The waitress brought our food.

I gasped when Christopher opened the door to our room for the night. He had prearranged with the hotel to have the room decorated. Hundreds of rose petals filled the room and were on the bed and on the carpet, and there was even a rose-petal path that led to the bathroom, where petals floated in a freshly drawn bubble bath in a claw-foot soaking tub. Chilled champagne and chocolate-covered strawberries were laid out on a cart next to the tub, rounding out the ambience.

"Wow!" I exhaled.

He led me to the bed, and I sat down on it. Still standing, he leaned down and kissed me. I wrapped my arms around his waist and kissed him back, feeling the fever between us. "See, there are ways I can be taller," he said when he pulled his mouth from mine and slipped my blouse over my head. "And horizontally, we're the same height." He smiled as he laid me back on the bed and took one of my breasts into his mouth.

The night was magical, and I felt full of love. More important, I felt loved.

The next morning in the bathroom, I peeled the wilted rose petals from my thighs and grinned as I caught the aroma of the sex from the night before. When I caught my reflection in the mirror, my grin turned to a full-blown smile. *I'm done; I'm quitting.* For the first time, I believed it.

CHAPTER 21

Mari and I passed notes at work like we were in seventh grade. In her first note, she invited me to San Jose again, but I wrote her back, letting her know I didn't need any more glue.

I'M DONE, I had written in all caps. Her reply was a lengthy line of question marks. This was getting difficult. I stood up, looked over the partition at her, and shrugged. Later on, during our break, she pleaded with me.

"I don't want to go to the farm alone! C'mon, please. Besides," she pouted, "I want to try to work things out with Mikey. Plus, it would be better if you were there."

"How so?"

"I don't know; it just would. C'mon, seriously, please!"

Her pouty mouth and distressed expression wore me down, and I agreed. I justified the decision by telling myself if I didn't do any of the drugs, I could sell them and make more money. I wasn't breaking my promise to myself. It made perfect sense.

After arriving in San Jose, we made our regular stop at the convenience store and bought our drinks for the cocktails. Mari laid out two little lines. My mind barked at me, reminding me that I'd decided to quit. She handed me the bill. My heart raced as my palms turned moist.

"Naw, I'm good."

"Suit yourself." She did my line in one breath and cranked the music. "I need to ask you something," she said, taking a long drink from her glass. "What are you willing to do?"

"What do you mean?"

"For Fuck-Face at the farm. I'm going to tell him off. That last time was a crock of shit, and I'm not having it again. It started with him just looking at my tits, you know? But then it was more and more … the touching and licking. Ugh!" She grimaced and slammed down her empty glass. "Bartender." I started fixing her another drink as she continued. "He's already seen your tits. Are you okay with that?"

"Um, I guess." I shrugged as I handed her a fresh cocktail and looked out the window. What else could I say?

As we drove, the signs of spring were everywhere; the fields were much greener than before, and there were blossoms on every tree. Life was beautiful. I really needed to quit the shit; there was more to life than being high. I was proud of myself for not giving in. Christopher's dimpled smile floated in my mind's eye. He was the one I wanted; I was sure. The thought made me grin.

As we approached the field, Mari flashed her headlights and got out of the car as my nerves escalated. It had been a while since we'd been here.

"You don't have to come," Mari conceded, noting my hesitation. "I'll get it if you don't."

"No, it's cool," I replied, walking beside her. My cocktail had been heavy, and I felt a little drunk.

Fuck-Face practically skipped toward the two of us. He put his arm around Mari's shoulders as they walked toward the warehouse like good friends, but their rapid-fire exchange in Spanish, coated in fake niceness, changed as soon as we got inside. Mari's tone turned firm, scolding, as she heatedly pointed at me and then back at herself. Fuck-Face smiled and nodded. She walked over to me, steeled by her plan.

"I told him he could look, but no touching," she said in a loud whisper as Fuck-Face motioned for us to remove our shirts.

As we complied with his request, he added something in Spanish as Mari sighed and reached around to unhook her bra. "He's insisting if he only looks, he has to see the whole chi-chi. God, I hate him," she complained softly as he held out his hands with another demand. I looked at Mari with a puzzled expression as she handed him her shirt and bra.

"He wants your shirt. He says he won't touch us, so …" This worked, morally anyway. No touching equals no cheating. Christopher was still on my mind. I handed Fuck-Face my top.

"Un momento, por favor." He rattled off one of the few Spanish phrases I knew, and my eyes darted back and forth between him and Mari as he stepped outside with our clothes and let out a shrill whistle. It reminded me of how my mother used to call my brother and me in for dinner—the ear-splitting kind made with fingers in the mouth.

The whistle had been a round-up call apparently, because within a matter of thirty seconds, all the farmworkers had lined up at the door. Fuck-Face let them in, one by one, allowing each worker to walk past us, appraising our bodies as if we were for sale. They pointed, talked, and laughed as Fuck-Face leaned against the wall, holding our clothes. He jeered at us, his nasty smile looking more predatory than friendly. Finally, the last man sauntered out.

"Tres," Mari spoke up, grabbing her bra from him.

"No puta, dos!" He laughed and threw our shirts and two bundles at our feet as he left the building.

"I fucking hate that man," Mari hissed as she dressed. We walked out to a chorus of applause, whistles, and catcalls as we rushed out to the car.

"Don't look at them," Mari instructed as we reached the car. "Motherfuckers. I hate them all!" She threw the car in reverse and sped away.

When we reached Mike and Patch's house, we were primed and ready to party. I still hadn't done a line but was getting drunker by the minute. We walked to the front door, and Mari knocked, but no one answered. She then twisted the doorknob. It was locked, but seconds later, we heard a rustling inside, and then the door flew open, revealing Patch.

"Hey, you're early," he greeted us, turning and moving to the kitchen.

"Nope, same time as always." Mari smiled. "Mikey up?" Patch nodded, and Mari disappeared into his room.

"How long are you girls here for this time?" Patch asked as he gathered the items to make a pot of coffee. I shrugged. "Well, do you mind taking the couch this weekend?" I shook my head, the energy between us awkward. "Cool, thanks."

After pouring himself a cup of coffee, he walked out of the kitchen, so I took my things to the living room to make myself comfortable on the couch. I poured a cup of coffee and wondered if I could make it the whole time here without doing any meth.

I switched on the television and was doing some channel surfing when a yelp came from Mike's bedroom. It sounded like Mari, so I turned down the sound, listening closely to make sure she was okay. Nervous laughter and pieces of conversation I couldn't make out floated into the room, quickly followed by a chorus of moaning and a creaking bed. A smile played across my face as I turned up the sound on the television. Maybe they'd made up after all.

By nightfall, I hated myself for giving in and doing a rather large line. Mari and Mikey had disappeared back into the bedroom. Patch had showered and left. Now I was spun out, by myself, and missing Christopher.

CHAPTER 22

Four days later, I sat at Kris's kitchen table, trying to cut the rock I'd brought back from San Jose, while Kris cooked biscuits with gravy and scrambled eggs for breakfast. As I worked, I noticed the window had been fixed and the house seemed normal, minus the husband, of course.

"Eat something before you do any of that, okay?" she encouraged me. "You're looking awful skinny."

"An added bonus." I laughed, continuing to crunch the rock into powder. "I'm not doing any. I'm done—quitting."

"Oh, don't do that!" Her answer surprised me.

"What? Why?"

"I don't want to be bad all by myself!" A Dr. Jekyll–Mr. Hyde smile formed on her lips, wicked yet cute at the same time. "But wait … can you give me some before you stomp it?"

"Sure." I slid half the powder to one side. "Is that enough?"

"How much for it?"

"A hundred bucks," I blurted out, surprised at how quickly I'd thrown out the number.

She rolled her eyes. "That seems steep. Fifty."

"No way. You owe me fifty from last time, so we'll say a hundred and call it even."

"Fine." She pouted as she served me breakfast. I put the other half of the drugs into a little vial and began to eat.

"So, Mari and her beau are back together?" Kris's tone was casual, but I could hear a hint of panic at the idea of no more glue.

"I guess." I forked a bite into my mouth and talked through it. "They were fucking five minutes after we walked in the door."

"Oh, that don't mean shit," she said between bites of egg. "People can just fuck, you know. If it feels good, do it, I always say." I contemplated that as she continued. "Speaking of … how's little Christopher?"

"Don't call him that!" I protested, giggling like a schoolgirl. "He's fine. We're going out tonight after work," I admitted, avoiding her gaze.

"Again? You're falling for him, Dacia! I knew it! I called it months ago." She took a triumphant sip of her coffee. "Good for you. Heaven knows you need a good man in your life. To be honest, you *sound* like you're in love."

I smiled. "The capital *L* word might be a tad steep. Let's say lowercase *l*. I definitely *like* him. He's nice … and cute. It's just … I don't know."

"He's short," she blurted out, stating the obvious. There it was, floating in front of me like a piss-yellow haze. "Don't be shallow, Dacia. That's like saying you won't date someone because they're black or Chinese."

"No, it's not that." She glared at me defiantly, and I felt defensive. "Okay, maybe I'm a bit hung up on his height."

"Get over it, for real. If that's the *only* thing you don't like about him, girl, please. You're an idiot if you don't go for it. When you go out, just pretend you're Christie Brinkley and he's Billy Joel. I don't think guys like Christopher come around all that often."

"Yeah, you're probably right." The thought of Christopher made me smile. He was growing on me. I looked forward to seeing him, and when I heard his voice on my answering machine, an involuntary smile came to my face.

"I *am* right." She cleared our dishes from the table. "And chop us up a little, if you're not quitting yet."

I looked at the pile of yellow powder sitting on the table. I didn't understand why the more I wanted to quit, the more I couldn't. Every time I told myself I was done, there was another pile of the shit staring up at me.

Chapter 23

I spent every night that week with Christopher. Not only did I enjoy his company, but I liked that I found it easy not to do the shit when he was around. I even had my schedule figured out—if I did my last line on my lunch break at work, I was actually tired by bedtime. I convinced myself this was the healthiest way to slowly wean myself off it.

Since our work schedules were completely different, we usually met at the bar for a few drinks. Some nights, he slept in my room at Suzy's, but mostly, I stayed at his house with him and his roommate, Cory. On the nights I got off early, we cooked together and rented movies from Blockbuster.

As we got to know each other, I discovered he'd been married and divorced and had a ten-year-old son named Jason. I had noticed the school portraits and drawings stuck to the fridge with magnets, but it had never dawned on me that they could be his child's.

"I want to meet him," I told him one morning as he got ready for work.

"Um. Maybe." He poured his coffee and mixed in a splash of whole milk.

"Maybe?"

"I don't know, Dacia." His voice was deep and serious. "I mean, I'm not sure this … this," he stumbled on his words, "whatever we have, this *whatever* is something I want my preadolescent son to think is an acceptable relationship."

At this comment, my lungs felt like a balloon that had been pricked a million times, oxygen leaving my body as my heart sank. I couldn't breathe. I cared about this relationship more than I thought.

"Don't be offended. Geez," he mumbled as he turned his attention back to his coffee. "You're fucking other dudes. Don't deny it."

"I am not!" Although I sounded defensive, I was telling the truth. I hadn't been with anyone but Christopher for quite some time.

Matt had been locked up for two weeks now, and Steve and I had slept together only one other time since the morning after the fateful concert. There had been a one-night stand with a cute college guy, but I didn't even know his name. I hadn't been with Patch in over a week, and in my mind, it hadn't really counted, since it had been so mechanical and emotionless. Besides, I knew he had other women he slept with, so it didn't really count, in my mind, anyway.

I took a deep breath and admitted to myself that "quite some time" was only days. I chose my words with care. "I'm not *dating* anybody else." That was more the truth. As far as actual relationships went, Christopher was it.

"Don't play me."

"I'm not."

My heart froze at the thought of not having Christopher in my life. I wanted to meet his son. I wanted to spend all my time with him. I'd even got earlier shifts at work so I could spend more time with him at night. He must have noticed the sincerity in my expression, because he set his coffee on the counter, wrapped his arms around my waist, and kissed my neck. I bent my head down and kissed him full on the mouth.

"When you stop fucking other dudes, you can meet Jason," he said with a grin as he caressed my butt.

"I'm done fucking other men," I said without a second thought.

He pulled my body into his, pressing his hard-on against my thigh. "I'll see what I can do, then," he agreed, kissing me on tippy-toes. "In the meantime, I've got to go to work. We'll address this later," he said, squeezing my ass with both hands.

I smiled. "You got it."

When I got to Suzy's, she met me at the door. "Hey," she said.

"Hey." I moved past her and up the stairs.

"You haven't been around much. You okay?"

"Yup." I kept walking.

"We need to talk." Her voice sounded tenser than usual. "You're not doing meth, are you?"

I stopped and turned to her, my face turning red. "What the fuck?"

"I'm sorry." She raised her hands in surrender, backpedaling a bit. "I read an article in the *Tribune* about meth use, and it seemed that you have some of the symptoms and—"

"What? Are you my mom now?" I knew I was getting defensive. "Do you want me to move out?"

"No. No! I just don't want my kids exposed to … um …"

"God, Suzy!" I stormed up the last few steps.

"And I need to get the rent!"

I turned and walked back down the stairs. "Here you go." I handed her the money. "For last month, this month, and half of next month." My words were clipped, and I didn't sound like myself. I wasn't mad at her; I was relieved. Between my fat paycheck and Kris's catching up with her tab, I finally had the money to square up with Suzy for the rent. I liked living here. It was one of the stabler things in my life. I recovered control of my emotions. "Sorry I snapped," I apologized. "I'm not doing meth," I said, a tiny moment of truth, as I wasn't high right then.

"It's cool." She put the money in the front pocket of her jeans. "Just worried about you is all. That's what friends do, you know?"

She smiled and headed into the kitchen; I dragged my butt up the stairs and sat on my bed. *I really am going to quit,* I told myself. *When this is gone, I'm done, for real this time.*

CHAPTER 24

As much as I didn't want to admit it, I was falling for Christopher, and I found it interesting how love made the world a bit brighter. We never got into arguments, we laughed frequently, and our relationship had all the qualities of friendship but with all the extra benefits.

Spring heated up to summer. With the longer days, I continued to take the earlier shifts so I could be off with Christopher in the evenings. For a while, I stayed at Christopher's every night, except on the nights he had Jason. I wanted to give them their space until Christopher reached a point where he could tell Jason about me. Thankfully, it only took a couple of weeks.

On a Friday morning, I remembered it was Jason's scheduled weekend to visit, so I said my goodbye to Christopher and told him to call me when Jason went home on Sunday. "I have a better idea," he said playfully, wrapping his arms around my waist. "How about a family-fun night at the Galleria?"

"Hm …" I stalled, leaning down for a kiss. "Does that make me family?" I reached out and touched his face—his day-old whiskers were rough against my hand. Our eyes met, and my heart skipped a beat.

"If you meet Jason, you're getting hella close."

"Close is where I want to be." I kissed him again and glanced at the clock. "You better run, or you'll be late." It sounded like something a wife would say, and it made me smile.

After he left, I grabbed my things and drove to Suzy's to switch my dirty laundry for clean clothes. Suzy met me at the door.

"Good morning," I said merrily. "Got your rent money upstairs."

"Rent? Seems like a high-priced storage locker." She laughed, following me up. "I've missed you. How are you?"

"Awesome!" I rummaged through my dresser and found my checkbook. "I've been seeing someone."

"Christopher from the club?" Her smile told me she already knew she was right.

"Yeah," I admitted, my face flushed.

"Doesn't it bother you that you're, like, six inches taller than him?"

"No," I lied. "It's closer to four inches, anyway." I handed her the check with a fake smile on my face.

"That would drive me nuts."

"You get used to it." I needed to change the subject, but thankfully, she did it for me.

"Oh, by the way, a letter came for you," Suzy informed me, pointing by my bed. "I left it on your nightstand. I think it's from Matt. The return address says it's from the county jail." She turned and sprang down the stairs. "Have a great day."

Glancing over, I immediately recognized Matt's heavy penmanship, a weird line crossing over his *t*'s. The line arced and dived to the right, ending in a sharp point. According to a magazine article I'd read, it meant he could be controlling and manipulative, with a sarcastic sense of humor. I found it strange that anyone could determine all that from one pen stroke. I reached for it and tore open the envelope—the postmark was two weeks old—and read the letter.

Dacia, or should I say traitorous bitch,

Why have you done this to me? I was nothing but good to you, and you repay me by fucking my best friend! Steve told me you practically raped him the morning after Mötley Crüe. Really? You do that while I'm sitting in a cold, dark cell that reeks of piss? You classless bitch!

He also told me that he told you about Angelique. Don't judge. Don't make assumptions. She blew shit out of proportion, and that's why I'm sitting here—because the women in my life are worthless sluts. I bet you're fucking that little pip-squeak too. You better not be, or else there will be hell to pay!

My attorney said I should be out by your birthday. I'm hoping we can still work things out. I know you didn't mean to fuck those other dudes. You have a sickness, like a sex addiction or something. But I'll always be there for you. You can always count on me.

I love you always,

Matt

As I read it, everything about the letter made my stomach turn. I rummaged around for a pad of paper and a pen and quickly scribbled a note back to him.

Matt,
Leave me alone. I don't judge and I don't make assumptions, but the hard truth is I'm not in love with you. In fact, I don't even like you, and I don't ever want to see you again. Forget my name. Forget my number. Forget my address. Don't come looking for me. There is nothing to work out.
I fucked Steve because his dick is bigger than yours. Live with it. As for the rest of my love life, it's none of your concern. As for Angelique, that's not my concern. I'm being serious. Leave me alone. I'm not above a restraining order.
Sincerely,
Your sex-addicted EX-girlfriend,
D.

As I signed the letter, an uneasy feeling settled over me as I thought of Christopher. In hand-to-hand combat, he wouldn't stand a chance against Matt, mostly because Matt would fight dirty. If it were a fair fight with a referee, Christopher might be able to hold his own. He was strong and small, so he would have good defenses. *Small.* There I went again with the size difference. *I'm so shallow,* I thought as I gathered my laundry.

Christopher and Jason were already at the Galleria when I got off work. There was a full-sized merry-go-round in the center of the room, its music blaring out of tune. Arcade games lined the walls, and a concession stand was near the rear exit.

Jason was a serious, somber-looking boy with big blue eyes and glasses that emphasized his round face. His straight blond hair contrasted with his dad's dark, wavy locks. "Hi" was all he said when his father introduced us.

After a quick dinner of pepperoni pizza, we bought twenty dollars' worth of tokens and headed to the arcade. Jason enjoyed the Cruis'n USA game while Christopher and I battled it out playing Tekken. Jason yawned as if a switch had been thrown when an employee announced over the PA system that the arcade was closing. I kissed Christopher and said good night to Jason.

"You're spending the night, right?" Christopher asked.

"Yeah, I'll be by in a bit," I assured him. "I'm going to meet Mari for a quick drink on my way back." My smile was sincere. "That way, you have time to get Jason down. Leave the light on for me."

Mari had been miserable the last two weeks. Her meth had run out, and she and Mikey were definitely done. She had asked me—no, pleaded with me—to sell her whatever I had left. Unfortunately, I couldn't help her. I'd sold most of it, and the little I had kept had been gone for over a week. I felt really good about being clean. My sleep patterns and my appetite had become normal again.

"What's up?" she asked as I slid into her booth.

"Not much—family-fun night at the Galleria." I motioned to the waitress.

"Sounds serious."

"It's getting there," I replied and gave the waitress my order.

After twenty minutes or so, Kristine showed up and slid into the booth on Mari's side. "I knew I'd find you here," she said as I raised an eyebrow in question. "Well, your car wasn't at Suzy's or Christopher's. This was the next logical place." I nodded in appreciation of her detective skills, but then her eyes sparkled.

"What's going on with you?" I asked. "You wouldn't come find me for nothing."

"I met a man!" Kris gasped. "His name is Daniel, and he is the absolute cat's meow." Her grin was infectious, and I giggled under my breath.

"And?" I encouraged.

"And I'll probably get laid this weekend." Kris and I laughed together as if on cue.

Mari clapped her hands together. "Well, there's some breaking news," she said sarcastically, tears filling her eyes. "At least you ladies are gettin' some." She stood and stomped to the bathroom, slamming the door behind her.

"What's up with her?" Kris asked me.

"They're done. Her and Mikey."

"Oh." Kris's eyes grew wide. "So … the glue is done too?"

"Um … he's not her hookup," I admitted.

"You've met her dealer? Will he sell directly to you?" I could hear the excitement building in Kris's voice. "If that's the case, we don't need her."

I rubbed my face, my eyes pinched tightly behind my hands. "It's just … um … she's … it's a delicate situation."

"What's a delicate situation?" Mari was back in the room.

"Well, I'm going to head out," Kris said abruptly. "Sorry to hear about your breakup," she offered to Mari and then turned to me. "I've still got a little if you want to have a girls' weekend next time your guy has his kid."

"We're totally in," Mari said. Kris scowled at her and turned her attention to me with an eye roll.

"He's got him now," I admitted. "I met him tonight. Jason is his name; he's a cute kid."

"Wow, you *are* getting serious. Good for you."

"How do you have any of that shit left? It's been two weeks!" Mari asked.

"Self-control, deary." Kris stood and got her purse. "So pencil me in next weekend, okay? We haven't had any best friend time lately, and I miss you." She emphasized the last syllable, and I wondered if Mari caught the subtle dig.

"Sounds good." I stood, hugged her, and watched her leave. Then I went to the bathroom to say goodbye to Mari.

When I got to Christopher's, I found him sitting at the kitchen table with Cory smoking a bowl of marijuana. Christopher kissed me passionately and laughed as he told me that Jason had talked about our night the whole way home. It was hard to picture, since the kid hadn't said two words all night. "He likes you," he said triumphantly.

Listening to Christopher's breathing that night, I felt truly happy for the first time since before I got married. Leonard felt like a lifetime ago.

CHAPTER 25

The night I had promised Kris a girls' night out, I met her at the club when I got off work. I didn't get there until after ten o'clock, and I could tell she was already buzzed when I saddled up next to her at the bar.

"There you are," she slurred. "Been waiting for you all night. C'mon!" She grabbed me by the wrist and steered me into the ladies' room. "Here." She handed me a bindle as we crowded into the handicap stall. It was fat—way more than I had expected.

"How do you save this stuff?" I asked. My body twitched with desire at the thought of a line, my hands moist with anticipation and my heart racing.

"Chop, chop, girlie," she instructed as she dropped her pants to pee.

"I'm quitting," I managed to say. With hesitation, I pulled a CD case from my purse, chopped two thick lines, and then slipped the bindle into my front pocket. She'd already rolled a dollar bill into a straw and snorted half of one line up each nostril. As I watched her, I wondered if I really wanted to do this. I'd been clean for a week.

"That's better." She winced after huffing up the fat line of powder.

But then, I couldn't help myself. There it was, again, staring me down. Doing the shit one time wouldn't hurt. I was in control of it, and if I kept it recreational, I'd be fine. I did my line—all in one huff up one side—and slipped the case back into my bag. "I'll meet you out there," I whispered as I slipped from the stall. When I reached the door, I heard her heave and throw up. I went back to our seats, knowing she would come back when she was good and ready.

"So much better," she stated when she returned. The scent of Doublemint gum lingered on her breath, and her newly applied lip gloss shimmered lightly in the dim lights of the club. "Do you have that little packet?" I nodded in affirmation. "Good. I thought I'd lost it," she mentioned as she sipped her drink and started talking about her new man.

"He's so different than you-know-who, but I like him! He's a great rebound, you know?" I nodded, agreeing with her. "Fantastic in bed too. And no kids." She raised her eyebrows. "That's a bonus, but then I think, *Do I want another kid?* Do you want kids?" I shrugged indifferently. "We should have a threesome with him."

My mind raced at the idea. When I did this drug, my sex drive was insatiable, but as my heart raced, I thought about my promise to Christopher—about him being the only one. But having sex with someone's boyfriend while she was there in the room could hardly count as infidelity. Or could it? When I was high, I lost all inhibitions, and I felt open to anything. Guilt ran in waves over me. If I were to go home with them, the sex would be like the drugs—recreational, for fun. It could be my secret too; it wasn't like Kris or Daniel would tell Christopher.

"Is he cute?" I heard my voice float out of nowhere.

"He's taller than you are."

"Well, that's a bonus." I smiled and took a long drink.

"How's Christopher doing?"

"Fine," I said, smiling.

"*Fine*," she said, her expression mocking me. "You're twitter-pated; that's that."

"*Twitter-pated* is a stretch," I pushed back, but if I were honest, I was beyond that.

When it was last call, Kris asked me, "So, who are we gonna fuck tonight?" She looked around the room, her pupils large and dark. We had put quite a dent in the bindle we had started with. My mind reeled. Taking some stranger home would definitely be a betrayal to Christopher.

"How 'bout your guy?" Hopefulness lined my tone.

"He's out of town this weekend. That's why this whole girls' night worked out. He'd probably freak out if he knew I was doing the shit."

"Christopher too," I said as we walked out the door.

"Christopher!" Kris's eyes lit up at me when we found her car in the parking lot. "What about him?"

"That's who we should fuck tonight." His tender touch and soft lips sprang to my mind. He *had* told me once that every man dreams of a threesome, right?

"Well," I considered, "okay. But let's do another bump before we go over there. I don't want him knowing we're doing this shit, okay?" She agreed, and we did another sizable line off the reliable CD case.

Parking across the street from his place, we darted in between the shadows to tap on his window. When he didn't respond, I rapped a bit louder. The bedside lamp came on, and his face appeared in the window.

"What the fuck are you doing, Dacia?" he asked sleepily.

"Meet us out front! I have an offer you can't refuse." I giggled.

"I'm tired."

"Trust me. It'll be worth it."

Kris and I made our way to the carport and hid in the darkness. For a minute, I didn't think he was going to come out, but then the door swung open, and he slipped out. I wrapped my arms around him and bent down to kiss him, but he wasn't having it.

"Don't be sore, baby," I whispered. "I was just hoping we could have a little loving."

"Why didn't you just come in?" he asked, noticing Kris for the first time. "We?"

"Wanna three-way?" I asked slyly.

He sighed, rubbing his hand over his face. "I highly doubt an opportunity like this will ever come again, so ... yeah, I guess I do."

"Don't sound so enthused," I deadpanned as he opened the door wider for us to go in. We followed him to his room.

"Cory's home and Jason's asleep in the guest room, so we have to be quiet," he instructed. Kris and I giggled and pulled our shirts over our heads.

"Okay." I kissed him with passion while I slowly took off his shirt. His breath hitched a bit as Kris pulled down his pants and took him into her mouth.

CHAPTER 26

The sun was coming up by the time we were done. As I said goodbye to him, he whispered, "That was amazing. Thank you." He kissed me gingerly and winked at Kris. We tiptoed out before the house woke.

Suzy was sipping coffee at the kitchen table when I came in. "Thought you were already home?"

"I am now," I said as I moved for the stairs.

"Looks like things are getting serious with you and Christopher."

"I guess," I agreed, avoiding her eyes for fear she'd see I was still a bit high.

"I heard on the news they may close your office."

"It made the news?" I asked, and she nodded, furrowing her brow in concern.

"You don't think you'll move, do you?" she asked as I shook my head in confusion. "It's just, I like you living here, and the extra rent money has been super helpful. Just … just give me at least a month's notice if you decide to move in with Christopher, okay?"

"I don't think you have anything to worry about. And of course, I'll for sure give you thirty days' notice."

"Okay, cool." She smiled. "He's a great guy, Dacia. You deserve someone that treats you well." I could tell she was as relieved as I was.

I climbed into bed, but my mind wouldn't stop spinning. I remembered Christopher would have his son with him this upcoming weekend, so I made a mental note to look at movies playing in the theaters that Jason might be interested in. Then my mind wandered to the bindle—how much of the eight ball had we done? I rolled out of bed, found the jeans I'd been wearing, and found it—it was three-quarters empty.

Dumping it onto the dresser, I divided it into three piles. I snorted the first pile and went to shower. No sleep for me today? No problem; I was beginning to think sleep was overrated. Although it felt euphoric to be high again, I mentally promised myself that when the three piles were gone, I'd go back to being straight and leave the shit alone.

As soon as I arrived at work that day, things settled into the normal routine, except that Joy took one look at me and sat on the other side of the sales floor. Then, later, Mari cornered me during my lunch break at my station. "Dee, are you high? You look high."

"I might be," I deflected.

She scooted closer. "Where'd you get it? Do you have more?"

"God, it was Kris's, okay. Leftovers from a month or so ago, if you can believe it."

"Got any more?" I shook my head fiercely as I thought of the two small piles on my dresser, praying she wouldn't ask for any.

"You've got to help me." She squeezed my arm, desperation dripping from her tone. "I need you to fly out and get us some more. Go to Fuck-Face and tell him it's for me, and then drive by Mikey's place and spy on him. I think he has another woman." Her voice cracked, the weight of this potential reality crushing her vocal cords.

"I don't know," I said, stalling. "Christopher has his son this weekend."

"Please!" Her voice sounded urgent now. "I just need more, okay! You can't judge me. And besides, I need to know once and for all if Mikey and I are done. Please, Dacia, I'll pay you. Whatever. Please." There was urgency in her pleas. "If you leave on the early flight, you can make it back later that day. Then you can have the best of both worlds: spend some time with your guy and his boy, and still help me out."

I begrudgingly nodded. "Fine."

"Sweet!" she squealed, clapping excitedly like a child. "I'll make it worth your time; I promise." She paused. "*Oh!* And I'll get you my keys. Freddie's in the back, so you can use the carpool lane. Thank you, thank you." Just the possibility of the drug turned Mari's whole attitude around. "Seriously, I owe you," she told me, but in my mind, I considered the irony of the money I could make from this deal.

Later, I told Christopher I had to work. Then I justified the lie by telling myself that selling meth was a part-time job, so the day trip technically *was* work. *Exactly,* I heard Mari's voice say in my head.

Everything went off without a hitch, and thankfully, I had no problem finding Mari's car or the exit for the farm. Fuck-Face recognized the car and smiled as he jogged toward me, but stopped when he saw Mari wasn't with me. Even though there hadn't been a line in the car, I was buzzed from a convenience-store Bloody Mary. I could handle this.

"Hi!" I said.

His eyes narrowed at my half-hearted greeting, and I watched as he stomped off toward the building. Eventually, I followed him, feeling like a scolded child, but seconds later, I felt more like his prey than a customer.

"What can I help you with?" he jeered in his broken English, circling me at a slow, measured pace.

"Well, you know …"

"No, I don't know." His circular pacing stopped when he faced me, undid the button on his jeans, and whipped out his hard penis, holding it in his hand. "How bad you want it, baby?"

My eyes drifted to the door and back to him, his sinister smile making my knees weak with fear. I calculated the odds of me being able to get to the door and out without him grabbing me. *This was a very bad idea,* I heard Suzy whisper in my ear. *You got this, girl,* Mari chimed in the other.

"Take off your clothes," Fuck-Face growled.

I complied out of fear but left my shoes on, and then he motioned for me to turn around. When I did, he moved behind me, pushed my head over so I was bent in half, and then slammed his cock into me. *Wel. Come. To. The. Mile. High. Club* went through my mind at each violent penetration. Then he pulled out, and I watched in disgust as his semen shot from between my legs and hit the floor. As I peered over my shoulder, witnessing the pure ecstasy on his face when he had finished, I wanted to puke.

As he reveled in his carnal pleasure, I grabbed my clothes and moved closer to the door, putting my shirt and shorts back on along the way. His laughter echoed through the room as he buttoned the fly of his work pants and handed me an eight ball.

"Four," I demanded, blocking him from the door. He laughed and kept moving, but I refused to budge. "Four, motherfucker!" I screamed, pushing him with all my might, causing him to stumble.

For a moment, his expression mimicked that of a dog when its owner threatens to beat it—a look of surprise, as if it can't believe you're threatening it, but then the expression transforms into one of fierce aggression right before it bares its teeth. I knew I'd crossed the line, but there was no going back.

"You heard me, motherfucker. Quatro." My tone was sarcastic and mean, and I realized how badly I wanted to do a line. It was so instinctive it felt primal. Every cell in my being wanted to huff a huge gagger, and the one package I held was not enough. The addiction rose in me so fiercely I heard the little devil on my shoulder applauding, cheering me on.

Surprisingly, my aggression worked! I watched in awe as Fuck-Face dug into his pocket and threw four bindles at my feet. I wasn't about to remind him that he'd already given me one. I scooped them up, turned indignantly on my heels, and stormed to the door, where it took me two attempts to get the door open. But at least he didn't follow me.

A shiver ran down my back as I briskly walked to Mari's car. When I looked back at him, he stared me down as I threw the car into reverse and drove away, the whole time chanting, "Fuck you, fuck you, fuck you," under my breath.

I quickly found a short, fat straw in the center console, and before I even merged back onto the freeway, I had shoved the straw into the first bindle and huffed, my eyes watering as the shit burned my inflamed nasal passages—anything to wash away the burning shame I felt. Since the drugs were in one big wad, tiny fragments of the yellow rock fell from my nose into my lap. I picked at them, put them in my mouth, and chased the flavor out with the leftover Bloody Mary in the cup holder as my body started to respond. My head tingled, my hands grew sweaty, and my heart raced as I merged onto the freeway and headed toward Mikey and Patch's place.

Mari had given me strict instructions to just drive by and check out the vehicles in their driveway, but since I'd lost all my inhibitions, I pulled into the driveway and parked. Several cars that I didn't recognize sat in the driveway. I smiled as I climbed out of the car. It wasn't even eleven in the morning yet, but music blared into the street, the window glass shaking with the rhythm of the thumping base.

I knocked hard—a "cop knock," as they call it. After a long minute, the volume got turned down, and Patch opened the door. His face went from a stern grimace to a horrified oh-my-god look. From his expression, and considering the fact I was driving her car, he'd obviously expected Mari.

"Hey." I smiled warmly, my body language entering into full-flirt mode. "Whatcha guys doin'?" He looked at me coldly, so I tried a different angle. "I just hooked up. Wanna party?" I tried, my mouth on autopilot.

"Hooked up?" Patch repeated, irritated, just as Mikey appeared at his side, pulling the door open a little wider.

"Hey, Dee," Mikey greeted me. "What are you doing here? Didn't Mari tell you we broke up?" As he spoke, I noticed several people, mostly women, milling around inside the house. But as I continued to look, it seemed like it was nothing *but* women.

"Yeah, I just came to get some shit—" I craned my neck, still looking inside.

"From Javier?" Patch's face turned red with anger as he looked to Mikey.

"I don't know his name … from wherever Mari gets it."

"What the fuck!" Patch screamed, raging like an animal. "How does she know about the family farm?"

"You should go." Mikey looked at me with urgency, his eyes wide and dilated.

"Mari and her fucked-up friends!" Patch screamed. He turned to the door.

"Seriously, you need to go, now." Mikey took my arm and pushed me out the doorway.

"Fuck this bitch," Patch roared, pointing at me as Mikey turned him back inside.

After moving Patch, Mikey pulled the door closed to limit my view and hissed, "And don't come back … ever." Then he slammed the door in my face.

I stomped back down the steps and got into the car, my blood boiling, and decided to do a proper chopped-up line. Retrieving the little mirror from the center console, I poured out some of the smaller rocks, proceeded to crush them, and then chopped them into a long line that ran the length of the case.

As I finished chopping the lines, I looked up to find a dark-haired woman staring at me through the front window. I then watched as she said something over her shoulder and Patch appeared. Ignoring them, I leaned down and huffed the line, and when I straightened back up, I flipped them the bird before pulling away.

CHAPTER 27

The drugs had made me brash, and when I got to the airport, I didn't even bother with the CoverGirl makeup cases or put the drugs in my bag. I left them in my front pockets and walked through security as if I was the most frequent of fliers.

When I got back to Salt Lake International Airport, I was so high I was afraid I wasn't fit to drive. I had done two bumps in the plane's restroom and then another little line in the bathroom at the airport. By this point, my paranoia had crept in; it seemed everyone was looking at me.

Even though it was after eleven at night, I put on my sunglasses, slunk to my car, and then sat there, trying to decide what to do. I wanted to see Christopher and Jason, but I didn't want Christopher to know I was high. I'd have to wait to meet up with them tomorrow. With that settled, I searched for a quarter to call Mari. When I found one, I walked across the airport's short-term parking lot to the pay phone. Even though it was late, she answered on the first ring, and we agreed to meet at my house.

When I got back to my car, I was surprised that I felt fine to drive, attributing it to the brisk walk across the parking garage. But once behind the wheel, I had second thoughts as the shadows created deep pockets of space and lights streaked across the garage with rainbows in the center. But what choice did I have?

Once I got started, the freeway seemed too daunting, so I took the back way through the residential streets. Finally, I arrived at my house and parked in my normal spot at the curb.

Mari scared the shit out of me when she appeared in my passenger window. As soon as I turned the engine off, she climbed into the car.

"Where have you been?" she hissed.

"At the airport."

"It's after 1:00 a.m., bitch! That flight got in at, like, eleven. Bust it out. C'mon already."

I looked her up and down and realized the stark contrast between her being straight and fraught and me floating in another world, unsure of what day it was. My rendezvous with Fuck-Face, Patch, and Mikey seemed like eons ago, but the desperation in Mari's face relit the burn of my shame. I tossed the open baggie into her lap.

"Thank you," she whispered, tearing it open and pouring the whole thing out onto a tray that she'd pulled from her purse.

"Shouldn't we go in?" I asked.

"Why?"

Her hands worked the rocks into a finer and finer powder, and instead of drawing a line, she took the straw and sniffed in random directions until she couldn't breathe in anymore. "So … did you see him?" she asked as she exhaled. I nodded, avoiding her gaze by looking out the windshield. "Fuck."

She handed me the tray, and I took it, still avoiding her eye, before snorting a random bit from the center and scooping it back into my vial. "You're splitting that with me, aren't you?" she asked.

"I have to charge you," I insisted as I filled my container.

"Sure, whatever." And sadly enough, I knew she *would* do whatever.

As I saw my own addiction reflected in her face, I thought of the four eight balls in my purse, and my stomach rolled in disgust. *I'm a horrible person,* I thought, the angel on my shoulder nodding in agreement.

"Naw, never mind, you don't have to pay me." I smiled at her as our eyes met.

"Thank you." She handed me an empty powder makeup case, and I scooped what was left into it as tears clung to her lower lashes. "Oh my god, you're the best. Thank you."

"Thirsty?" I asked. She nodded, and I climbed out of the car. "Be right back."

I headed to the backyard, calling the dog's name under my breath. He came up to me, wriggling and happy to be petted. I thought of Matt doing the same thing when he used to sneak into my room. I opened the back door, retrieved two beers from the fridge, and headed back out, where Mari had another line waiting for me. We did it and drank the beers, and I snuck in and got two more.

That night, as Mari and I talked, snorted, and smoked in my car until the sun started coming up, I made an odd connection that linked to my childhood. Even though I had never been fond of nicknames, my parents had nicknamed me Gabby Gertie as a kid because I loved to talk. And as I sat there, enjoying myself, I inwardly laughed that there would've been no way for them to have known that, as an adult, the nickname would become even more fitting, because when I was cranked up on meth, I was like the Energizer bunny; I just kept going and going, talking and talking.

As usual, the sound of bus brakes made me realize how late—or, shall I say, how early—it was. "Shit, hide," I instructed. Mari looked at me as if I were dumb when I reclined the driver's seat, but I hid as Suzy's kids walked in front of my car and climbed on the bus, and Mari waved away. "Fuck. Busted," I muttered.

"Hey, you're a grown woman. If you want to sit in a parked car with another grown woman, well, as weird as it sounds, you have that right." She took a toke from the pot pipe.

"Shit, dude, put that away. Someone could be watching us!" I positioned the driver's seat back upright and looked around at the neighborhood waking up around us.

"Paranoia could destroy ya," she sang as she got out of my car. "See you at work."

Mari sauntered off as I went into the house, where Suzy had been waiting for me, her eyes livid. "What the fuck was that?"

"What?" I matched her confrontational tone.

"In the car, with that … that …" My eyes narrowed, waiting to see how she'd finish the sentence. "Mari," she said, spitting her name out as if it were a rotten piece of fish. "I'm not going to lie, Dacia. I don't like her."

My mind swam. I was so high that I could literally feel each individual hair tingling and standing up on the back of my neck.

"You're not my mom," I yelled as I stormed up the stairs, feeling immature for my outburst.

"Keep your druggie friends away from my kids!" she screamed.

When I walked through my bedroom door, the answering machine blinked with new messages. The first one was from Christopher. Fuck, how could I have forgotten to call him?

"Hey, Dacia, what time are you off tonight? Call us. I'll leave the light on for you and the back door unlocked. Jason and I can't wait to see you."

In his next message, he sounded disappointed. "Hey, it's bedtime. If you get this, I hope to see you. Call me."

The last one was worried. "Hope you're all right. Let me know what's up when you get this."

I chided myself as I dialed his number. He picked up on the third ring. "You okay?" he asked.

"Yeah, I'm fine." I took a deep breath, and thankfully, he didn't sound mad. "Just a little mandatory overtime last night. It was late when I got home, so I just crashed."

"You working today?"

I glanced in the mirror at myself and saw how high I looked. "Um, yeah, time and a half," I heard myself lie.

"Aw, that's a bummer. Jason was looking forward to going to the movies with you this weekend. Call me when you're off."

I assured him I would as I opened another bindle and chopped some of the yellow rocks on my dresser.

CHAPTER 28

Later that afternoon, I found a letter from Matt on the stairs. As I scooped it up, my shoulders tense, I grabbed a pencil, slashing a line through my name and address. I scribbled *Return to sender* across the front and dropped it back in the mailbox. Since I didn't have to work, I called Mari. "You really going to work today?"

"Funny you should ask; I was thinking of taking a vacation day."

"I don't have to work today," I said. "If you did take a vacation day today, I could take one tomorrow, and we could go to Vegas." My jaw worked back and forth, grinding my teeth, as I waited for her answer.

"How much more shit do you have?" she asked.

"Enough."

"Well, let me call and see if I can get a vacation day, and I'll call you right back." I smiled as she hung up the phone, knowing we were going to Vegas.

The phone rang eight minutes later. "We're set," she said and proceeded to tell me about the flight times and standby availability.

"Okay. You come get me so we only have one car."

"Sounds good," she replied, and we disconnected.

I scraped a good amount of the yellow powder into a makeup container and hid the other eight balls in a folded pair of socks, then stuffed them in the back of a bottom drawer in my bedroom.

Within minutes, I packed my two favorite outfits, an extra pair of panties, and a toothbrush into my bag and waited for Mari. In less than an hour, we were in her car, driving to the airport.

Being a tourist was never my scene, so when I went to Sin City, I skipped the Strip and partied at Fremont Street in what was considered Old Town. My favorite place was a two-for-one bar; one side had a Jamaican vibe, and the other side was a blues bar.

Our night melded into a laid-back party, fueled by meth and booze. We made out with men we had just met, but I refrained from having sex with them, my mind racked with guilt. I was high and drunk and groping a man I couldn't care less about. I wanted Christopher. What was I doing here? Again and again, I told myself, *I'm quitting; I'm done.*

CHAPTER 29

When we got to work on Monday, Mari was called into our boss's office as soon as she clocked in, which was never a good sign. Her face was blotchy and her eyes were rimmed in red when she returned.

"What was that about? You okay?" I whispered.

"Uh, no. Far from it." She avoided my gaze. "They, um … they suspended my flight benefits."

"What? Why? What for?" I asked.

"Well, remember when I called in for a vacation day on the day we went to Vegas?" I nodded, prodding her to continue. "So, there wasn't a vacation day available, like I told you, so I improvised and told them I was sick instead."

I sighed. Of all the things she could have done. In our company, there were very few ways to lose flight benefits, but using flight privileges on a day you'd called in sick was the first way to do it, and resulted in immediate suspension.

"I didn't think they would find out." Her voice cracked. "They're gonna fire me if I don't get my shit together."

"Then get your shit together." My mind flashed to the rumors of our company getting bought out by the airline. "Don't let it go down like that. You got this!"

She smiled at me, but her smile didn't look convincing. "Well, I brought that stuff you gave me. Let's go out to my car and do a bump," she suggested.

I considered her offer. The line was mine in the first place, since I had given it to her, and because there was no way I'd make any money on it, I decided to take her up on her offer.

Even though I was high all the time, I managed to get through my week at work without any attendance issues. I vacillated between being okay with my drug use and feeling shame and guilt over it. Mari, on the other hand, had asked me to call her every day and wake her to make sure she was on time for her afternoon shifts.

We regularly did lines at our seven o'clock "lunch break" and then more when we got off work. Most nights, we were able to catch last call for a cocktail or two before doing more lines in the parking lot. Then we did more as we hung out in my room or parked in front of Suzy's. That seemed to be our preferred place since we could smoke herb and laugh loudly in my car. When the sun started to come up, Mari would leave to go home and try to sleep, and I would slink up the stairs and do more shit. *I'm quitting; I'm done.* Those words seemed to be white noise in the background of my drug-addled mind.

Since I hadn't slept for three nights, I wasn't too keen on seeing Christopher, as there was no way he could see me and not know I was high. So instead, I called him each day and left a message when I knew he was at work. He called back twice when I was at work, and I wondered if he was deliberately calling when he knew I wasn't home.

Looking in the mirror, I could see the meth damage to my skin and hair. I had taken up the unattractive habit of picking sores on my arms. Some days, I just couldn't let them be and would scratch, dig, and squeeze the open wounds for hours. Long sleeves were my only option; my arms made me look like I was a leper. I'd lost so much weight even my shoes went down a size. I was in denial, telling myself I was perfectly fine, functioning like any other normal adult.

Mari ended up buying an eight ball before she finished the partial one I'd given her. Since she didn't know I had two more, she was "being conservative" with what she had, but she had started to mention how badly she'd need me to go back to San Jose to get more. I assured Mari I would take care of her, which set her mind at ease. I could see the panic in her eyes when she thought there might never be more. It was easy to lie to her. I was lying to everyone else in my life, from my boss to Joy to Suzy. They all got the same response to their concerns: "I'm fine, just tired; that's all."

I had busted into another eight ball, and I swore to myself I would sell every granule of the last one. As I huffed a huge line, the little devil on my shoulder whispered at me, encouraging me to hang on to what I had. So, I devised a plan; since Mari and Kris were technically my only customers, I plotted on charging them for the shit but having them do the majority of it with me. I would make some money and still get high, all while delaying my trip to San Jose.

Toward the end of the week, Kris left me a message that she wanted to have dinner over the weekend, and she asked me to let her know which night worked better. When I called back, she didn't answer, but I left her a message saying that Saturday would work best. Then I called Christopher and left him a message that I had missed him and would like to see him later Saturday night. If he didn't call back to confirm, I rationalized I could just drop by his place when I was done at Kris's, and if he wasn't home, I could probably catch him at the club.

When I arrived at Kris's house that Saturday, the smell of roasted chicken and other lovely aromas made my stomach growl. I hadn't eaten much all week except for a couple of bites of peanut butter.

"This smells wonderful!" I complimented her as I surveyed the spread: roasted chicken, mashed potatoes, and a hot, bubbly blackberry cobbler for dessert. "I'm going to wash up before we eat!" When I came out of the bathroom, where I had indulged in a little predinner bump, I offered her a line. She seemed impressed I still had some, but there was no need to tell her it was a different bindle than the one I'd split with her, I told myself.

"I'll pass for now—don't want to ruin my appetite," she explained as she bustled around the kitchen.

The doorbell rang, and Kris asked if I'd get it. My eyes went wide as I opened the door.

"Hey," Christopher greeted me, "I thought I'd catch you here!" He wrapped his arms around my waist and stretched up to kiss me on my cheek. "Damn, girl, you're gettin' skinny," he said as he patted my ass and walked into the kitchen.

"Hey, Christopher!" Kris said enthusiastically. "You're just in time! Want to join us for dinner?"

"That sounds delightful," he responded as Kris handed him a place setting. I felt light-headed at this exchange; it felt rehearsed.

During dinner, although the food smelled and tasted good, I was too high to fully enjoy it. After we'd cleared the table, Kris sat back down and exhaled a long, heavy sigh. *Here we go,* I thought.

"Dacia, we're concerned about you," Kris started. At those words, my head snapped in her direction. Then I looked at Christopher, staring at his folded hands. I shook my head at Kris, pleading with my eyes for her to stop. I didn't want her saying anything about the shit in front of Christopher. "You've lost a lot of weight, and for all intents and purposes, you look like shit."

"Fuck you," I said. A wave of defensiveness washed over me as I glanced at an unmoving Christopher

"We care about you and are concerned about your addiction prob—" she started.

"*My* addiction?" I spluttered. "Really? It's *my* addiction? You do the shit too, you hypocritical bitch," I accused her, my heart pounding in my chest. This was not a conversation I wanted to have in front of Christopher. They exchanged looks.

"Well …" She sighed again. "We just care about you and your—"

"What's this *we* shit?" I looked at Kris and then at Christopher, then watched as Kris slid her hand toward him. Christopher reached out and clutched her hand, tears brimming in his eyes. Unable to help myself, I reached over and took his other hand. We looked like a polygamist family ready to offer prayer.

"Are you okay?" I whispered, trying to get him to look at me. He avoided my eyes. A single tear rolled down his face.

"We're in love," Kris said flatly. It took a few seconds for the words to settle as Christopher let go of my hand and covered his eyes, emitting a gulping noise.

"What? We? Who?" I asked her, even though the answer was obvious. "I'm sorry. I must be confused." My eyes darted between them. "What happened to the cat's meow?"

"Daniel? That was more of a fling; you understand all about those one-nighters." She winked at me and forced a laugh. "Dacia, we care about you and don't want our," she said as she pointed to her and Christopher, "relationship to interfere with the friendship between all of us. You mean a lot to both of us."

"What relationship is interfering with what friendship, exactly?" I said, refusing to believe what they were telling me.

At this point, the room slanted a few degrees to the left as my focus on Kris blurred around the edges. I could see her mouth moving, but her words were disconnected and didn't make sense. I looked at Christopher; he held Kris's hand as tears silently streaked down his face.

She was still speaking when my ears adjusted to what she was saying. "Just because Christopher and I are involved doesn't mean we don't have your best interest at heart. We want you to get professional help because we care about you. And, more importantly, we want to make sure our friendship remains intact."

"Involved?" My brain couldn't keep up.

"Christopher moved in last weekend. Like I just said, we're in love." The word hung there between the three of us. Define *love*.

"What about when we all … you know? Who cared for who then?"

"It was the beginning of a beautiful relationship." Her eyes held mine, but her hand remained tightly around his.

"I'm sorry," Christopher finally choked out, but Kris cut him off.

"Sweetie, we agreed we wouldn't apologize for the way we feel," she reminded him.

"I'm not apologizing about how we feel! I'm apologizing for the way I'm making her feel. I had no intention of hurting anyone's feelings." He turned and looked at me. "You and I were a … um … I don't know." He sighed and looked back at Kris.

"Temporary," Kris chimed in. "Our relationship has a foundation for something bigger than a few wild weekends and a roll in the hay."

"That's what I was to you?" I gasped at him. "A roll in the hay? A piece of ass?" My emotions were getting the best of me.

He shook his head, clearly upset. "No, but that's what I was to you."

CHAPTER 30

Slamming the door of the house and then my car, I revved the engine and drove away. I knew I shouldn't have been driving, but I couldn't stay there with them. At the stoplight, I rummaged through my bag and grabbed a small bindle of meth, snorting it right from the paper. Then I stopped for gas, found a pay phone, and called Mari, leaving a message that I'd be at the bar when she got off work.

When I arrived, I ordered a double and deliberately sat on the stool that was unofficially Christopher's.

"You okay?" Doc asked, to which I nodded and downed half the drink.

Thankfully, because of the combination of the drugs, the half a joint, and the alcohol I consumed, I was finally numb enough to process the atomic bomb that Kris and Christopher had dropped on me just as Mari appeared at my side. I looked down at my watch, shocked that it could be so late.

"No, I left early," she explained, filling in the gaps. "I told work there had been a family emergency. How are you?" Concern turned her mouth into a frown, not knowing exactly what was wrong, just that I was upset.

"They are gonna fire your ass," I said, taking another drink, wanting to stall as long as possible. Telling her would make it too real.

"Don't worry about me. What's up with you? I thought you had plans tonight with your lover boy."

"I don't have a lover boy anymore." I raised my glass in a toast. "Here's to the single life." I tapped her beer with my glass.

"Did he find out about the shit?"

I nodded and contradicted myself. "They're in love, they're concerned about me—"

"Wait. What?" Mari's forehead knit into a frown.

"You heard me right; they're in love."

"Those fucking assholes," she said.

"So, you wanna do a line?" I asked her.

"You have more?" Her delighted tone was all I needed to hear. We went into the bathroom and finished the bindle I had found earlier.

"That was a tease. Is that all you have?"

"Nope." I smiled, and after the last call, we found ourselves back at my place, where I broke out the fourth eight ball.

"Oh my god, sell this to me!" she demanded as she huffed a four-inch line off the mirror on my dresser. "How much you want for it?" I shrugged as puzzlement washed over her face. "Wait … did you go back out there?" I ignored her and bent down to snort my line. "So, you've had this the whole time?" she pushed. I didn't respond, and my silence confirmed the answer. "How many more do you have, honestly?"

"That's it," I lied, knowing there was one more.

"So, split this with me, and fly out and get another round. Fuck-Face obviously likes you *way* more than me because he would *never* give me more than two."

My face flushed at the thought of my last rendezvous in California. "His name is Javier, by the way."

"How do you know?"

"Patch."

"What? You talked to Patch?" she stuttered. "When? Why?"

"When I was out there." The apprehension on her face sent a chill down my spine.

"Did you talk to Mikey?" I knew that the truth would upset her, so I lied and said I hadn't. We raided Suzy's fridge for the wine and headed out to my car to smoke a joint.

"What are you going to do about the Kris and Chris show?"

I shrugged. "Get over it, I guess."

We stayed up until after the kids went to school and then napped in my room for a few hours and did another line before work.

CHAPTER 31

Joy and I sat next to each other. She could tell by my voice something was wrong. "I don't want to talk about it," I told her when she asked.

"You need to make an appointment with me. We can get rid of all that negative energy you're carrying around."

"I don't have any negative energy," I denied. "I'm happier than I've ever been."

"Uh-huh." She rolled her eyes. "How about next Friday?"

I agreed just to end the conversation.

When I got off work that night, I headed to the bar. In my mind, I pictured Christopher sitting on his regular bar stool and walking toward me, telling me his affair with Kris had been a huge mistake. Then he'd kiss me, whispering in my ear how badly he wanted to make love to me. But my fantasy was shattered as soon as I walked through the door; his bar stool was empty.

I sat down and placed my hand on the old, crusted leather seat where he should've been sitting. Doc set a drink in front of me and then motioned to the set of booths on the opposite wall. I turned and looked. There they were, leaning in close to each other, as Kris fed Christopher peanuts from the dish on the table—just like a Roman servant would feed the king his grapes. They smiled and giggled with each other. I slammed the drink back, paid Doc, and walked back out, feeling like I was going to puke.

At home, I found a note on the stairs.

> I don't know what's going on, but your phone rang so much today I had to turn the ringer off again. Sorry. Hope everything is okay.
> Love,
> Suz

I had nine messages waiting for me on my machine, and when I scrolled through the caller ID, I had more than fifty missed calls.

The first one was from Kris, rambling on about how sorry she was, how important I was to her and Christopher, and how she hoped we would all be friends someday. I pushed delete before the message ended. The next one was the recorded voice of the county jail requesting I accept a collect call. When the recording for the name came on, Matt screamed at me. "Accept the call!"

The third call came from Kris, inviting me to meet her and Christopher at the bar after work. I hit delete. The fourth and fifth calls were again from the county jail. "This is a collect call from," then Matt's voice saying, "Damn it, Dacia, answer! When I get out—"

"Press 1 to accept the charges," the computer voice cut in.

My heart sank.

Then there was another message from Kris, calling from the pay phone at the bar. "We're here!" she sang. "Got a booth. Hope to see you soon!"

I got up and found the last bindle of meth and opened it as I listened to the last three messages, all the automated voice of the county jail and then Matt, professing his love for me in short eight-second spurts.

As I leaned down to snort the line I had just laid out, the machine picked up. It startled me as I heard my prerecorded message, "You've reached Dacia. You know what to do. You know when to do it," followed by the beep. For a split second, I wondered why my phone hadn't rung, but quickly remembered that Suzy had turned off my ringer. This time, it was Christopher.

"She didn't answer; it's the machine," he said.

Following a muffled sound, I could hear the buzz in Kris's voice. "Dacia, come down here this minute. Doc said you came in but you left. Where are you? Don't be mad at me, please."

"C'mon, babe!" I heard Christopher cooing to her in the background. "Let's go."

The line went silent. I huffed the line and pushed play on the machine, erasing all the prior messages until it got to the last one. I listened to it again, and again, and again, tears rolling down my cheeks.

Chapter 32

I did most of the eight ball over the next four days, not sleeping at all. Taking advantage of the nighttime hours, I cleaned my room, organized my closet, detailed my car, and then scrubbed the bathroom I shared with Suzy until it was spotless. I was moody and cried often, but I honestly couldn't decide whether I was depressed or I just needed sleep and food. Either way, I hated myself for not being in control of the drugs. *Addiction.* The word haunted me. I couldn't wait for the bindle to be gone, but then I panicked when I thought about it being gone.

On the morning of my appointment with Joy, she called at about dawn. Since Matt had been calling at least four times a day, I had left my ringer off, but the machine indicated my incoming calls when it picked up.

Joy's voice sounded chipper and bright. "Good morning, lovely lady," she said.

I grabbed the receiver and tried to sound like I'd been sleeping. "Hey. I'm here."

"Oh, sorry if I woke you, but I have bad news. I need to reschedule our appointment today."

"What!" I feigned disappointment. "But you—"

"I know, it's the strangest thing," she said and sighed, "but when I think about you, I get physically ill."

"What! I don't ..." I stumbled, not knowing what to say. "Physically ill?"

"I don't understand it either, but I know the heavens are trying to tell me it's not a good time to work on you. How about Sunday morning around eight?"

"Um, I guess." Tears welled in my eyes.

"You're still wearing that necklace; I can feel it over the phone. Dacia, bury it. Return that stone to Mother Earth." Reflexively, I reached up and held the stone. "So, Sunday, early. See you then. Toodles!" She disconnected before I could speak. I dialed Mari.

"What's up?" she asked, her words weighted with sleep.

A flood of emotion, tears, and snot exploded from me. "I made Joy, the psychic lady, sick!" I cried.

"Who? Joy? Sick? How?"

"I had an appointment with her this morning, but she just called and canceled on me! She says when she thinks about me, she gets sick … like *physically ill* sick."

"Fuck that bitch," Mari said. "Calm down. You'll be fine! You're going through withdrawals. Just focus on getting on that plane and getting us some more glue. It'll hold our lives together … for real." She giggled at her own joke. "Don't let that wacky woman get under your skin. I'm going back to sleep."

To an extent, she was right. I took a deep breath. It wasn't withdrawals I was going through, but I did need some sleep and food. *I'm done; I'm quitting.*

"Okay, you're right," I agreed as I calmed down. "I'll leave first thing tomorrow morning and be back by the afternoon, okay?"

"Sounds good. See you soon."

I kept one large line for my trip to Salinas and finished the rest of the eight ball.

Since Mari's car at the airport had actually been Mikey's and was no longer available to use, I had to rent a car when I arrived in San Jose. I did the line and bought two mini bottles of rum, mixing the rum with a fountain Coke.

Pulling up to the farm, I flashed my lights at the workers as always. A couple of them glanced my way, but none of them approached. I got out and waved my arms above my head in an overexaggerated greeting, trying to spot Javier. I stood there for a bit and then started to walk toward the cluster of farmhands and noticed Javier standing among them.

"Hey, man. What's up?" He looked at me, a blank expression on his face. "Hey, man. What's up?" I repeated, glancing at the other workers. None of them acknowledged me.

"No hablo Ingles," Javier answered without a hint of an accent.

"What the fuck, dude?" I asked, panic rising in my chest.

"Get the fuck out of here," he threatened.

"What—" I began, but he cut me off.

"You got a real big mouth, missy. Now go."

"I didn't think you spoke English," I shot back, realizing how immature I sounded. I turned to head back to the car, but Javier grabbed my arm. "That hurts!" I shouted as I attempted to twist away from him.

"You almost got me fired, you little cunt," he growled at me. "I don't *ever* want to see your face here again, and if you even think of running your mouth to Patch, I'll silence you forever. You got that, bitch?"

Confusion turned to understanding as he released my arm. I ran to the car, glancing back once to be sure he wasn't following me.

Driving to the airport, I dug through my purse, looking for more meth, but I only found the empty makeup container I'd planned on filling. I ran my tongue all around the sides and top. My mouth watered at the bitterness. Tears filled my eyes as I drove at eighty miles per hour back to the airport.

When I got back to Suzy's, I realized I'd only been gone seven hours, to California and back in less time than a day's work. I paced the length of my room, trying to decide what to do, and Kris came to mind. I bet she still had some shit stashed, but I wouldn't give her the time of day, let alone plead for a hookup. So, in desperation, I dialed Steve's number.

"Hey, buddy, it's me," I greeted him when he answered.

"Who?"

"Is this Steve?" I asked, now uncertain.

"Dacia?"

As soon as he said my name, relief flooded me. "Yeah! Long time, no talk. How are you?"

"What do you want?"

"Um, just calling to say hello."

"Yeah, I'm calling bullshit on that," he said and sighed. "Is this about Matt getting out this weekend? I don't think they're going to release him. The whole thing with Angelique is going to go to trial."

"No, not at all." This was new news.

"You're a good girl, Dacia. Do me a favor and stay away from him. You deserve so much better."

This wasn't going well, so I knew I needed to act fast. "Um, Steve, you don't know where to get any of the … um … icky stuff, do you?"

"Oh honey, no. I've been clean for over a month. Stay away from that shit. It's the devil walking." Hearing me sigh, he continued. "For real, it's the black plague of modern times. You're better off without it."

"Maybe," I said, my voice cracking.

"There're no maybes about it. Seriously, that shit is bad news."

I began to pace the room as he tried to convince me to give it up. After a few more minutes, I assured him I'd stay clean and hung up.

Every couple of minutes, I would rummage through a drawer or box, looking for the tiniest bit of the yellow powder. As I searched, I found a wad of crumpled-up paper and a bunch of little scraps, and I started going through them, unfolding them one at a time. One of the scraps contained the phone number from Jack, the guy I'd slept with on my birthday all those months ago. On the third ring, someone picked up.

"Jack?"

"Nope, Scott. Who's this?"

Scott? The white-jeans dude? "Oh, just a friend." There was a long pause while I debated what to do, but then Scott's voice interrupted my thoughts.

"What kind of friend?" The playfulness of his voice made me grin, despite the anxious feeling in my gut.

"Aw, a friend with benefits, I suppose. I met you a few months back. I stayed over on my birthday?" It came out as a question.

"Oh yeah! Tall blonde with the smokin' hot roommate, if I remember right."

As irritating as I found that comment, I acknowledged him. "Yep! That's me. Anyways, just looking for some shit, you know?"

"Seems like everyone is dry, dry, dry, from what I understand." He paused. "Jack is on a quest for some of that sticky, icky glue as we speak. If you want, grab a six-pack and come on over, and we can wait together."

"Really? Sure!" I knew I sounded overly eager, but the possibility of relief transformed me into someone else—someone who sounded more addicted than I would ever admit. "Be there soon."

CHAPTER 33

In my dream, I found myself next to a river, its fast-paced current captivating me as the froth and bubbles roiled over and around the rocks. A fishing pole and a white Styrofoam cooler sat near me. When I looked into the cooler, a beautiful fish floated there, its gills shimmering in the sun, changing from pink to green to silver and then back to pink. I noticed a fishhook stuck in its mouth, connected to a small, bloody thread, so I gently removed the hook from its mouth. It wiggled, grateful and happy to be free.

Don't worry. I'm not going to kill you, I silently assured it as I stood, picking up the half-filled cooler. As the water sloshed out onto my shirt, I startled awake. I found it difficult to breathe. The cord of my necklace was squeezing in on my throat. Clawing at my throat, I woke for real.

The sun inched around the window covering, and I panicked as I noticed curtains; my room at Suzy's place had blinds.

Where the hell am I?

Brief flashes of the night before popped into my head: the beer, a few shots of tequila, a phone call, kissing, Scott pressing me against the wall as he pulled off my pants and suckled my breasts with passion.

I pulled the necklace over my head and took a deep breath. Fumbling, when I set it on the nightstand, my hand brushed against something. I looked over and saw two condoms on the nightstand, still shiny in their foiled wrappers. An image appeared of me getting them from my purse before Scott carried a naked me down the hall to his bedroom. Panicking, I tried to remember when I'd had my last period, and I tried to estimate the timing. My birth-control pills had run out the week before, and I had meant to make an appointment to get them refilled, but days had turned to weeks, or had it been a month? Months?

A fog lifted when Scott rolled over and slid his arm around my waist, pulling me close. But at the movement, I slid away from him, literally jumping from the bed.

"What part of 'I'm not on the pill' did you not understand?" I screamed as I stormed out of his room in search of my clothes.

"What the fuck?" I heard him mutter as I strolled into the hallway.

Glancing out the front window, I realized Jack hadn't come home, which meant there was nothing to get high with. My heart sank as my stomach flipped over; I was going to be sick. I rushed to the kitchen sink in time to heave up green bile into it as Scott walked in behind me.

"What's your problem?" he asked, his voice groggy from sleep.

"You! You're my fucking problem!" I shouted, snatching my pants from the back of the couch and pulling them on with harsh, determined movements.

"Dude …" He sighed. "Chill out! Jesus Christ, Dacia, don't go all psycho on me." Scott turned and went back down the hall and into the bathroom as I finished putting on my clothes. By the time he returned, I had gathered everything except the two condoms and my necklace; those I left on the nightstand.

"I'm leaving. Just have Jack call me, okay?" I turned to leave, my shoulders tense with irritation.

"Um, fuck you too."

At that, my whole body snapped. "No, seriously, you little fucker, have Jack call me."

I stormed out, but a lump formed in my throat and tears stung my eyes when I heard the door slam behind me. I really wanted a line. It had been over forty-four hours since I'd finished my stash in the rental car. When was the last time I had gone two full days without the shit? Before the Kris and Christopher betrayal, maybe a month, five weeks at most? I dug through my purse, hoping to find a hidden line I'd somehow overlooked. No such luck.

The clock in the car read 7:38 a.m., and it struck me that it was Sunday. I had my appointment with Joy in twenty minutes! I steadied myself and closed my eyes. Little snaps of light pinged off the backs of my eyeballs. I knew it was just withdrawal, but it made me uneasy. Subconsciously, I reached for the stone of the necklace. I looked back at Scott and Jack's house, thinking, *I'm done; I'm quitting.* The little devil argued, *You could probably get it back when you see Jack.*

As I drove to Joy's house, I thought about the last conversation I'd had with her and hoped she hadn't tried my phone to reschedule again. But even more than that, I hoped the thought of me wasn't making her physically ill.

When I pulled into her driveway, it wasn't quite eight, so I turned the car off and waited, truly feeling my body for the first time in a while. For this little stint, I hadn't been high on meth in two days. I reckoned in the last six months, I hadn't been high only thirty days—on average, once every six days. Embarrassment, shame, and worthlessness crashed over me. I felt a lump in my throat as if I were going to cry.

The popping sensation behind my eyelids had stopped. I closed them and took several deep breaths. When I opened them, I almost jumped out of my skin. Joy was standing right by me, her face bent down to the window. "Didn't think you'd show up," she said when I opened the car door.

"Here I am." I sounded much more sarcastic than I intended, but Joy just smiled and put her arm around my waist, steering me into her living room.

"Coffee?" she offered, but I shook my head no. "Were you up all night?" I shook my head no again and gave her a quizzical look. "Nice. You're not lying to me this morning."

"I don't lie."

She raised one eyebrow and laughed. "Sure you don't. Instead of debating the question of your honesty, let's go ahead and get started."

She led me into a bedroom that had been converted into her therapy room. "I'll utilize some massage techniques, combined with the gathering of your angels, to clear your aura. Let's work with you lying faceup. I'll be right back."

As I got settled, I took in the room; the yellow walls with pink accents created a bright yet calming effect as the morning sunlight streamed in through the sheer white curtains. I stripped off my clothes, leaned back on her massage table, and adjusted the sheet to cover me. I breathed deeply and smelled the incense that was burning on a little corner shelf. Joy's feet hardly made a noise on the hardwood floors. I could hear her moving around the little house.

When she returned, I couldn't believe what I was witnessing. Holding two large feathers in her hands, she had applied some sort of makeup on her cheeks that looked like war paint, and after she pushed play on the CD player, Native American music flooded the room.

Joy proceeded to bob around the table, lighting several more incense sticks. She then picked up a large seashell and removed a smudge stick of sage. When she lit it, the dry herb flared, causing a thick plume of smoke to rise into the air. The smell instantly took me back to a memory of camping with my family as a child. Thoughts of my mom cascaded over me.

When Joy started chanting along with the CD, I shut my eyes so they wouldn't betray my giggling. I literally tripped out when I opened them again. I was looking down *at* myself, as in I could literally see all my body on the table. I closed my eyes and shook my head again, only to see the same thing when I opened them. I was floating, hovering right below the ceiling.

Oddly enough, my first reaction was that of surprise, not because I was having an out-of-body experience but because I saw how thin Joy's hair was. I could see her pink scalp peeking through her pink strands of hair as she hopped and danced around my body, screeching and howling along with the Natives on the CD.

CHAPTER 34

From up above, I studied my face, and although it struck me how pretty I looked, the dark rings under my closed eyes were noticeable. I panned out and took in the room as a whole. The sheet that hung off the table outlined my body—at one point, I'd been athletic, toned even, but now, I was nothing but skin and bones.

Letting out a loud cry that sounded like a hawk, Joy startled me, causing me to jerk up and out, beyond the ceiling and into a bright gold light as I felt something indescribable.

The words *I am your guardian angel* came into my subconscious, even though I saw no visible being and heard no real sound.

Oh, I am tripping! I began to giggle as a booming laughter joined me.

No. You don't believe me? I felt the words again.

Then the laughter transformed from joyous to menacing as two bright streaks of light appeared on either side of me, racing toward each other like comets ready to collide. As they neared each other, shapes formed, and the streaking light turned into two open hands, crashing together to create a thunderous noise, then silence. I watched in awe as the hands opened and I was pulled into the scene unfolding in the palms of those huge hands.

I saw the dog from my baby scrapbook. I didn't remember this dog, but I recognized her from the photo album, which had several pictures of me with her. The words *Dacia and Lizzy* were printed below each of the photographs in my mother's neat handwriting. In one picture, I was riding on the back of the dog as my young mother laughed. In another, the Saint Bernard curled around my small form as I slept.

I watched as another scene played out in front of me. My mother, resting on a towel reading a magazine, jumped up as the phone rang. In two long strides, she snatched it from the receiver, and when she laughed, the sound mimicked a bubbling brook. I studied her face; she was just a baby herself as my mind did the math. If she was eighteen when she had me and I was toddling about with the dog, she had to be about twenty or twenty-one, so young to have so much responsibility.

Then the dog barked loudly. My mom stretched the phone cord as taut as it would go and leaned out the door. "Hush, Lizzy!" But the dog barked again, an urgent sound.

My attention moved from my mother to the dog, pacing with irritation by the back corner of the fence. Toddler me was on the outside, toddling down the road. The energy of light by me pulsated near a gap under the fence. The dog tried to get through but couldn't fit, so the balled light inched the fence up so the huge dog could get through.

By the time my mother hung up the phone and realized I wasn't in the yard, the dog and I were four blocks away, the traffic swerving around us. The light showed me how it rode the dog as it followed me, protecting me from the traffic.

I watched as a car zoomed past, blaring its horn as another car approached slowly behind the Saint Bernard. "Lizzy?" It was my aunt. My aunt had recognized the dog and pulled over, but what a shock for her when she saw me toddling along the ditch in the bank.

As the story went, Lizzy wouldn't let my aunt pick me up, nor could she bribe the dog to get in the car, so she parked and started walking me back toward my house. We were only one block closer to where I lived when we saw my panic-stricken mother jogging toward us. This particular story became legend in my family, my mom recounting multiple times over how the dog had saved my life that day.

In the next scene, I had fallen from a teeter-totter when a flash of light streaked under my body and turned me ten degrees so that I fell on my shoulder instead of directly onto my skull.

In the next scene, my mother and I were at the ER, where the doctor told her, "Well, she couldn't have landed any better. There is no indication of a head injury, and her back is fine too. She is one lucky little lady."

In the next scene, I rocked big hair with blue eye shadow and matching eyeliner. I had snuck out to hitchhike to a local carnival. A man had pulled over on his motorcycle. The stench of booze on his breath about knocked me over, but I still hopped on.

As he exited the highway for the event, the motorcycle collapsed under him. He slid with it, but the arc of light curled under each of my armpits, placing me gently on the asphalt. I scrambled to the berm on the side of the freeway and watched the man tumble, his motorcycle careening on top of him.

I stayed hidden while the ambulances came and scooped him up, the tow truck gathering what was left of his bike. Once they were gone, I rushed to the other side of the freeway and found a bus stop to go back home. I watched as I lowered myself into my basement window just as my parents' alarm went off, beckoning them to work.

The show continued—me at sixteen, my new car packed full of teenagers, music pounding from the subwoofer. Going too fast down a hill onto the freeway, I rounded the corner and watched as large balls of light went up into two of the tires as I cranked the wheel onto the on-ramp. My gut knotted as I remembered my fear, thinking I would surely roll. The lights smashed into the outside of the car, and I realized every teenager in that car had had a guardian angel pushing the car to make sure we landed back on all four wheels as I downshifted and roared onto the freeway.

Scene after scene played in this mammoth set of hands, all the way up to the night before. I watched as Scott carried me down the hallway, the two condoms gripped in my hand. The thunderous laughter returned.

Again, a loud clap made me jump, and suddenly, I was in a casino. The generic *bling-bling-bling* noises and bright lights flashing around me caused me to feel dizzy. A roulette wheel started spinning before my eyes, enhancing the nausea. The roulette dealer was a large, beautiful black man. He had a dazzling smile and dancing eyes, but didn't speak. With a clap of his hands, he set the white marble in motion.

Red is death, black is jail, or is it black is death and red is jail? The unspoken voice came again, and my brain spun. Death? Jail? My eyes followed the marble as it danced and hopped over the spinning wheel. My stomach dropped as my head spun. The roulette wheel slowed, and the ball settled into the double zero: green.

Winner, winner, we've got ourselves a winner. My eyes floated up, and I made eye contact with the roulette dealer. He was smiling, his chocolate-colored eyes reassuring, loving, merry. I couldn't help but start to grin.

Suddenly, the floor opened below me, and I fell back into Joy's therapy room. The Native screams of the CD still played as she stood near my head, her hands cupped over her eyes, her head thrown back, her makeup smeared into a mess. The room, overpowered by the smell of the incense and sage, glowed as the ball of light came up from behind me and completely enveloped me.

You are loved. It was no longer the incomprehensible voice of the spirit that claimed to be my guardian angel; it was my mother's voice, soothing and soft in my ear.

I looked down as a black tarlike substance flowed out from my abdominal area. My body twitched and jerked on the table as this happened, until no more darkness flowed out of me. Then my spirit was gently placed back into my body. I could feel my mom's presence near my feet, the golden light hovering over me as Joy told me she would now repair the damage to my aura.

A pink light came around me, starting at my feet and moving up past my chin, curling toward my face. My guardian angel laughed again and then dropped a small blazing light on me. It slid into my face, right in the midst of the pink aura. Like a zipper, the energy cocooned my physical being, closed around me. It was bright and pink. I inhaled sharply as the ball of glowing light settled into my uterus.

CHAPTER 35

The aura cleansing had been a success, Joy assured me, and other than experiencing some mild exhaustion, I should feel fine. She hugged me before I left, whispering, "The universe has big things in store for you." I didn't tell her about my experience in the casino or about the bundle of light that had entered me.

By the time I merged onto the freeway, my body heaved with sobs. My plan was to go home, pack an overnight bag, and head to Vegas, where I knew I'd be able to find the day-after pill that was new on the market.

My sobbing had settled by the time I parked in front of the house. I had a plan, and everything would work out fine. I hadn't taken two steps toward the house when I was grabbed from behind. I screamed and flailed my arms, striking my attacker hard in the side of the head.

"Whoa, whoa, whoa." The man released me, and I spun around to face Christopher.

"What the fuck?" I turned and started toward the house.

"Dacia, please. Talk to me. I really am sorry," he said, his smile disarming me. "Especially the way it all went down—"

"Fucked up," I snapped.

He nodded slowly and took a seat on the porch and then patted his hand next to him, an invitation to join him. "Yeah, not the way I was hoping to handle things." He casually put his arm around my shoulders, and I leaned into him and took a deep breath. His scent relaxed me, allowed me to briefly forget the last twelve hours. Things were going to be fine, and for the first time in a while, a hint of a grin threatened to spread across my lips.

"We got married last weekend," he confessed.

"Who did?" My spine straightened as his words sunk in.

"Kris and me. Who else?" He grinned as my smile turned to a grimace. At that moment, I could think of nothing else but how badly I wanted to hit him.

"Is she pregnant?" His broadening smile was the only answer I got before the front door opened.

"The phone is for you," Suzy told me. Confused, I stood and walked toward her on autopilot.

"You can be mad at me, but you're Kris's best friend. Don't take your anger out on her," he said from behind me. "Let's just all stay friends, please. I'm asking as nicely as I can. She misses you."

"Whatever," I said as I crossed the threshold into Suzy's house and half-slammed the door. She thrust her cordless handset into my hand. "Hello?"

It was my brother. Without prerequisite, he blurted out, "Are you okay?"

Confusion swirled around me. "Sure, why wouldn't I be?"

"I don't know, sis. I had a dream last night about you and …" His voice cracked. "Um, Mom told me to check on you—in my dream, of course. She looked so good, so young. When I told her you were fine, she got angry and yelled at me to call you. She told me that you needed a big brother, that you needed your family. I've been trying your line all morning and finally called Suzy out of pure desperation." I glanced at Suzy, who was doing a great job of pretending she wasn't paying attention. I took the phone to the front porch, where only moments ago I had been seated with Christopher.

"I think I'm pregnant," I said so softly I wasn't sure my brother had heard me.

After a heartbeat, he answered, "Aw, that's great news." His voice was soft and full of love. "Just what this family needs—a baby."

"What are you talking about?" Tears welled in my eyes and spilled down my cheeks. "I'd be the shittiest mom on the freakin' planet." For a moment, a twang of guilt stabbed me in my gut; he and his wife had been trying to get pregnant for five years, but his laugh was supportive and kind.

"I think you'd surprise yourself, sis."

With that, we disconnected, and I slunk up the stairs.

"You okay?" Suzy called after me. I nodded and burst into tears.

Once in my room, I threw myself onto my bed and sobbed. When the tears began to subside, I got up and kicked my beanbag chair. My foot went right through the fabric, and the chair stuck to me like a huge glob of Styrofoam. I kicked and thrashed, causing the little foam beads to fly through the air, and when the chair released from my body, I threw it violently. My room looked like an upturned snow globe.

"What?" I screamed when I heard a small knock at the door. The door cracked open slightly, and Suzy let out a little gasp. "I'll clean it up," I promised, but then I noticed Mari standing next to Suzy. As Mari entered, Suzy pulled my door shut and went back down the stairs.

"What's up?" Mari ignored the foam beads swirling and settling around the room. All I could do was shake my head. She sat next to me on the bed and put her arm around me. "Did you find any glue?" I shook my head harder, covering my face with my hands, and began to sob. "Well, it's not that big of a deal. Geez. Seriously, girl, what's going on?"

"I think I got pregnant last night."

"What? C'mon, why would you think that? Don't think that. Seriously."

I shrugged. "I don't know—wrong time of the month to not be using protection? Um …" Our eyes met. "Some other, uh, weird stuff." I didn't want her to know I had been to Joy's house, and definitely couldn't tell her about the out-of-body experience.

"Who were you fuckin'?"

I sighed. "Does it matter?"

"Ah, yeah, especially if you're pregnant."

"Mari!"

"Okay, it doesn't matter. You can tell me later. Maybe we should call your mom."

"My mom is dead," I cried and bent over, putting my face back in my hands.

"What? How did I not know that? Seriously, we've stayed up and talked all night many times, and you never mentioned your mom had died."

"It never came up?" I mumbled through wet fingers.

"I know her favorite gum but didn't know she had passed away? What is wrong with me?" she said more to herself than to me, then added, "I think I have a pregnancy test in the car."

"What?"

"Yeah, I thought I had a bun in the oven a month or so ago and bought a two-pack. The first one was negative, and I didn't want to tempt fate, so I never used the second one." She got up and headed toward the door.

"It hasn't even been twenty-four hours."

"Those things can tell the minute you're pregnant apparently, with all those cells snappin' and poppin'." She snapped her fingers at my face, and I was reminded of the electric energy that had burst around my head when I had left Scott's.

Without waiting for a reply, she headed to her car and returned with an EPT test a minute later, tossing it into my lap. Unwrapping it, I handed her the directions and headed to the bathroom.

Three minutes later, I walked out, looking down at the second line, which was faint but definitely there. I handed the test to Mari. She took one look at it and started screaming and pacing my small floor. "Oh fuck, oh fuck, ah! It means you're fucked!"

I snatched the paper from her hand and looked at the directions—two lines meant a pregnancy. "Fuck," I said under my breath.

"Maybe we should call your dad. Is *he* still alive?"

"Maybe you should go." I put my arm on her shoulder, steering her toward the door.

"Call me later, or call Planned Parenthood. Are you okay to work? Holy shit, a kid." She spun and threw her arms around me. "You'll be a great mama if you decide to keep it," she said and sighed into my ear, "but you didn't hear that from me."

Once she was gone, I went to get the vacuum to clean up the mess I had made.

CHAPTER 36

Taking Mari's advice, I called Planned Parenthood the next day and was promptly connected with a nurse once I explained my situation. She answered my questions regarding the day-after pill. She also confirmed I could get it in Vegas.

"But you don't have to drive all that way. The clinic in Wendover has it available, as it's legal all over Nevada. That's only a ninety-minute drive, sweetie. I can call ahead for you and let the clinic know you're on your way." I agreed, so she took down my information to give to the clinic in Nevada and then gave me the address to the clinic.

Getting my backpack out, I threw in a pair of sweats, two T-shirts, a pair of underwear, and some fuzzy socks. Work could schedule my last vacation day. I told Suzy I'd be back and headed north on I-15 to get on I-80 West.

As I moved along, the traffic seemed heavier than usual, but I knew I needed to switch lanes, or else I'd be forced to exit in downtown Salt Lake. Looking in my rearview mirror to make a lane change, I saw the traffic plotted against me. My eyes welled with tears.

What am I doing? I asked myself but then clearly heard a reply. *Winner, winner, we have ourselves a winner.* Were balls of light hitting the cars around me, or was I imagining them?

I had no other choice but to exit, and I found myself in downtown Salt Lake City as tears poured down my face. I glanced at the clock and did the math. I'd been off the glue for three full days. As I drove up and down the streets of Salt Lake, I decided to chalk up the incident at Joy's to a hallucination, and the confusion and sweating I blamed on *delirium tremens*, or DTs, a term I'd pulled from the recesses of my brain from my old high-school health class.

Even though I had no destination, I felt guided by some invisible force. Near

LDS Hospital in the Avenues, I parked in front of a Victorian-style house with a sign in the yard—The Aspen Charter House: Alcohol and Substance Abuse Treatment Center. I blinked hard, assuming it was another vision, but the sign didn't move. Forgetting about Planned Parenthood, I got out of my car and walked up the sidewalk. It was Sunday, so part of me didn't expect their door to open when I tried it, but it did.

The receptionist was perky and cute, her smile reassuring. "I need help," I choked.

"We're glad you came in." She handed me a clipboard containing the patient intake forms. As I filled them out, my hands shook so badly my handwriting was indecipherable.

When I handed the forms back to her, she asked me if I had chemical-dependency coverage with my insurance. "No clue."

"What's your employee number? I'll check the system and see if I can find out." She handed me a pen and a sticky note for me to jot down the information. "In the meantime, I'm going to have our nurse come get you, and we'll take some vitals and get you settled in."

"I've got to be at work tomorrow." I sounded pitiful as a wave of nausea washed over me. I sat on the cushioned chair and bent over, cupping my face in my hands.

"Dacia?" A deep male voice with a sexy texture to it called out my name, and actually pronounced it correctly. I looked up into caring blue eyes and an empathetic expression. My nurse was quite a cutie, and I became aware of myself. I wiped snot into my hand and onto the back of my pants as I stood. "I'm Dean Martin. I'll be helping you out today. Are you doing okay?"

I shook my head and let him lead me down the hall and into an exam room. "Dean Martin?" I asked.

"What can I say? My mom loved the classics." His eyes twinkled when he mentioned his mom.

Once I was seated, he took my blood pressure and noted it was high. "What are you coming off of?" His tone was even, his stare hard but caring.

I shrugged. "I think I'm pregnant."

He sighed and looked away from me. "Look, we're glad you came in, but you didn't stagger in here because you think you're pregnant. You've got to be honest with me."

Disappointment washed over me when I saw a ring on his third finger. I looked up and felt busted when I realized he'd noticed what jewelry I'd been staring at, but he refused to back down or be distracted.

"So, what is it, Dacia? Heroin? Meth?" The color drained from my face as an understanding dawned in his eyes. "God, do you have any idea what's in that shit?" he scolded me, writing it down in my file. He held out a calendar to me. "When did you use last?"

Tears blurred my vision as I looked at the calendar and avoided his stare. "Three days ago." My voice sounded as if it were coming from a different room.

"How far along are you?" I shrugged. "When was your last period?" I pointed to the date on the calendar. "Well then," he said, brightening, "you're probably not pregnant unless you had unprotected sex in the last forty-eight hours." My head dropped, and a sob escaped my lips.

"It's going to be okay, Dacia, really. Whatever you decide as far as your pregnancy goes is up to you. Regardless, let's get you some rest and some food and take care of *you* so you can make some rational decisions, okay?" He put his hand under my chin, forcing me to look at him. "Most of what you're experiencing right now is due to withdrawal. I'm going to recommend you stay here a few days and dry out, okay? Are you with me?" I nodded. "Good!" He took the rest of my vitals, had me sign another form, and then walked me down another long hallway to a different room, where the original receptionist met us.

"Oh, great news!" she informed me. "You have a full recovery plan on your work insurance, so rehab will be completely covered!" She was so cute and excited I couldn't help but grin.

She showed me to the private room that my insurance covered. The room was frilly and girlie; the quilt on the bed reminded me of something my grandma would have made. "Get some sleep," the perky receptionist suggested and then left me to get settled.

I quickly changed into the sweats I'd brought from home, and as I eased into bed, Mari popped into my mind. *She really should join me here before she gets fired,* I thought.

With thoughts of Mari swirling in my head, I fell asleep in thirty seconds. Sometime after dark, I awoke to the smell of food and found a cheese sandwich with mayonnaise and butter and a cup of chicken broth in my room. I scarfed it down like an animal, my stomach gurgling in pleasure, and then went back to sleep.

This went on for a few more meals: biscuits and gravy, macaroni and cheese, and something else—chicken and chocolate cake? I don't remember. My mealtimes were hazy. Sometimes a nurse was there; other times I woke to find the food on the bedside table.

One morning, I was awake when a young woman in a frilly pink-striped apron opened the door and brought in a tray of food: a ham and cheese omelet with toast and jam. She bustled around me, filling a water glass and popping a straw into it.

"Thank you." I paused, feeling silly. "Do you know what day it is?"

"The nineteenth." Her smile was warm and kind.

"I've been here a whole week?"

"Eight days," she confirmed.

"What have I been doing all week?" I asked as I took a bite of the food.

"Sleeping."

CHAPTER 37

My time during the in-house rehab vacillated from it feeling like an expensive spa to it feeling like a high-security prison. I talked on the phone a lot. My mom once said I was born with a phone in one hand and a camera in the other. The idea of it made me smile.

Suzy and I talked on a daily basis, and I was grateful for her friendship and support. My sister-in-law called me on occasion, since it was long distance. It felt good to have family worrying about me. She told me about her life being married to my brother, her career selling real estate, and their idea of adopting or fostering a child since they still hadn't been able to get pregnant.

In order for the insurance to pay for 100 percent of my treatment, I had to sign a form agreeing to complete six months of an outpatient drug and alcohol recovery program upon being discharged, or else I'd be billed for the entire treatment and lose my job. Part of my outpatient treatment plan also included attending weekly Narcotics Anonymous meetings. I went, but they were too "godly" for me. I just couldn't buy into the whole "let go and let god" thing, but I attended anyway. I couldn't miss a meeting without being on my deathbed. Plus, I had to stay clean for more than just me. The pregnancy was already making itself known through morning sickness and a heightened sense of smell.

When I came home, Suzy rushed up to me and threw her arms around me. "I've been so worried about you." I smiled. "You look good," she added. "Clean, sober." I nodded. Nothing else was said about my absence.

When I went up to my room, I found forty-two messages on the machine. I pushed play and listened to the first few. Matt, Kris, Matt again … Without thinking, I unplugged the machine and walked it to the trash can on the side of the house. Cellular phones were just coming into the mainstream, and I thought of doing some research on getting one.

Returning to work after being gone a month, I thought someone would ask questions or wonder where I was. No one did, except Joy.

"Welcome back!" she gushed. "How are you?"

"Been better, been worse." I smiled.

"Well, you look good."

"Thanks."

Once I logged in, I immediately looked up Mari's schedule for the day but couldn't find her name. I checked the schedule for the next day, but she still wasn't listed. After scanning through four or five more days without seeing her name, I asked a scheduling supervisor about her. "She's not here anymore" was the matter-of-fact answer.

I dashed to the phone bank and dialed her number only to get an automated message stating that the number was no longer in service. With a furrowed brow, I walked back to my cubicle.

"Looking for Mari?" Joy asked. "They fired her. Last week." She exhaled as I sat down and faced her. "I was here when it happened. The union reps escorted her to her car, but she made such a ruckus they threatened to call security."

"Fired? For what?" My mind reeled as I wondered if I'd be able to find her again.

"Dacia"—Joy put her hand on my knee—"she's a drug addict."

In that moment, it seemed as if the floor shifted below my feet, and I wanted to scream out, "But I am too." Mari was no different than me. But having felt like I'd been punched, I couldn't find the oxygen to utter those words.

"I'm glad you were smart enough to avoid getting wrapped up in all that nonsense." She then turned and went back to the phone. "Morris Air, Joy speaking. How may I help you?" If only she knew.

I thought of my answering machine sitting in the bottom of Suzy's trash bin. Maybe when I got home, I could retrieve it and play the dozens of messages and find one from Mari.

But as I took call after call, the idea of *not* contacting her settled over me. Perhaps it was time I made a clean break from her, as hard as it was for me to admit. Even though Joy had been wrong and I *hadn't* been smart enough to not get wrapped up in all the nonsense, I would be smart enough to stay straight and take care of my baby. *My baby.* The idea of it was nutty—becoming a mom, having a human being completely rely on me. Yeah, I needed to get my shit together. The vision of the answering machine being dumped into the landfill renewed my intentions to stay sober.

I hadn't told a soul about the pregnancy. Not Scott. Not Suzy. I had told my brother when I had thought I might be pregnant, but I'd never confirmed it with him, and obviously, the staff at the Aspen Charter House knew, but doctor–patient confidentiality agreements wouldn't allow them to tell anyone. Heck, they couldn't even tell anyone I'd been there at all.

Time unraveled throughout the waning winter. At one of my doctor's appointments, I heard the baby's heartbeat. It was so fast I couldn't even keep up. It sounded like hummingbird wings. I asked the doctor, "How do you know that's not my heart?"

"If your heart was beating that fast, you'd be dead," he told me.

I thought of the number of times my heartbeat had pulsated at my temples when I'd been high, when I could physically feel the blood coursing through my body. The memory made me shiver. On the one hand, I felt grateful I'd been clean for a few months. On the other hand, my body still craved the nasty chemicals.

During the Narcotics Anonymous meetings, I learned what was in the shit I'd packed up my nose, and it frightened me and disgusted me at the same time. I learned the chemicals were extracted from things such as brake cleaner, engine starter, rubbing alcohol, and fertilizer. I blanched at the idea I'd been high on those chemicals, touching my stomach in a physical gesture to remind myself as to why I wasn't going to have more.

I sat in the same cubicle day after day, hour after hour, answering the phones. My stomach grew; it looked like I was hiding a basketball under my shirt. The merger between the two airlines caused subtle shifts in policy, but for the most part, things remained the same.

One afternoon, Joy walked up to me and asked, "Did you get a pink slip?"

The day had come when I'd find out whether I was going to remain employed. Before becoming pregnant, I wouldn't have cared one way or another. Now with my baby due in only a few months, the paychecks and insurance were a vital component of my success. Whether I liked it or not, I needed this job.

I shrugged, trying to seem indifferent. "How do I find out?" I asked.

"Your supervisor should have let you know by now. Go check your memo box." The memo box was a series of hanging folders on the main sales floor. Each of us had a folder with our employee number on the top. With shaking hands, I opened the folder. Empty. I looked in the folder in front and back of mine. Tears welled in my eyes as I realized I had managed to stay employed through the company merger, rehab and all. Tears began to run down both cheeks as the reality of providing for another human being settled over me. This job would give me what I needed to be a good parent.

"Oh my god, Dacia. Are you okay?" It was my supervisor. "I'm so, so sorry," she consoled me, putting her arm around me. This kind gesture caused my early pregnancy hormones to kick in even more. My shoulders shook, and I sobbed.

She steered me into her windowless office and closed the door behind us. "How did you find out?"

"Well, there's no pink slip in my folder," I blubbered.

She looked at me, puzzled. "I meant about Mari," she said, and then it was my turn to look confused. "So you haven't heard about Mari?" she asked.

I shrugged. "Joy told me she got fired."

Our eyes met; hers looked sad. "She was killed this morning in a car accident." For an instant, the air got sucked from the room and I couldn't breathe as she continued. "She wasn't wearing a seat belt. Her blood alcohol level was over the legal limit. Her dad called me—"

I grabbed the small trash bin beside her desk and vomited up green bile and decaf coffee.

"Oh my god!" she shrieked and then stood to offer me a box of tissues. "I'll grab you some water."

The small office seemed to get smaller. The ceiling came closer to my head. I vomited again in between my sobs. Mari dead. The thought crashed into my heart as memories cascaded into my mind's eye. The grin that never let you know whether she was pissed, her casual way she loved those around her, the times we sat up all night talking about music or where we wanted to travel, her tears over Mikey. My hands rested lightly on my stomach. My last memory of her was when I had done the pregnancy test. She had been with me when I found out I was going to be a mother. It didn't seem real that she could just be gone. I wondered if she had suffered, if she had been in pain. What were her final words? Did she cuss? Cry?

My supervisor returned and handed me the water as she grabbed the trash can. "You think you're done? I should probably rinse this out." I nodded yes and wiped my nose. We talked for a few minutes before she sent me back to the phones.

As I sat down, I thought back over the morning and realized with certainty that no one knew where I'd been the entire month, especially after the comments from Joy and my supervisor. My supervisor had said that all she had known was that I'd been out on medical leave, and then she proceeded to ask me about my health after I'd puked. *Thumbs-up to confidentiality,* I thought. For an explanation, I admitted to her that I was pregnant.

As I drove home that night, the sunset was spectacular. I thought of Mari, that faraway look in her eyes. The words my angel had offered me in the imaginary casino came back to me: *Black is death; red is jail.* Or had it been the other way around? Either way, Mari was gone. Dead. I shook my head. Just then, the baby rolled in my stomach, reminding me of life—precious life.

Then I thought of Matt. Jailed. My stomach rolled. I could never tell him I was pregnant, and from a one-night stand, of all things. A prisoner—Matt was a prisoner. If I had gone to jail, my baby would be born there. Social services would surely take it away. It would wind up in foster care or be offered up for adoption to strangers. I got lucky. My roulette ball had hit the green. I got another chance, a baby. That led me to worry about another small hitch. What *was* I going to tell people? I would start showing soon. There was always the truth. I thought of Christopher, and my heart felt heavy.

CHAPTER 38

I knew I had to tell Scott I was pregnant; it was the least I could do. I didn't know his last name but vaguely remembered where he lived.

After driving up and down the block I thought he lived on, I spied a couch pulled to the road with a handwritten For Sale sign on it. It was Scott's couch. I pulled up in front of the house and noticed a For Rent sign in the window. The door was open. I could hear a vacuum running under the loud music blaring from the living room.

I saw boxes of Scott's belongings stacked near the doorway and by his car. The boxes were labeled *kitchen*, *bedroom*, and *bathroom*. I picked up the black marker from the top box and looked around for something to write on. I considered my arm before pulling up my shirt and scrawling the phone number off the For Sale sign onto my stomach.

The windows of his cherry-red Camaro were down, and I glanced in to see his wallet in the center console. I glanced at the house. The vacuum was still running. I opened the wallet and saw his driver's license picture staring up at me, alongside his full name and birthday. I raised my shirt and wrote his birthday, October 12, that was about the time the baby was due. *Ironic*, I thought.

I opened the wallet farther until I found his social security card. I pulled up the other side of my shirt and began writing the sequence of numbers on the other side of my stomach.

"What the fuck are you doing here?" His voice sounded cold, hard, and pissed. I jumped and let my shirt fall back into place. His social security card floated to the ground.

Panic swept over my face. "Hey, Scott," I managed to say. His eyes dropped to my hand holding his open wallet. He snatched the wallet from my hand

and stooped to pick the card off the ground. There were black blotches on my fingertips. "I'm pregnant," I said, staring at the mess on my hands.

"So," he said and moved back toward the house. As if it took the words a few seconds to sink in, he slowed and stopped on the top step of the porch. "You're not here to suggest it's mine, are you?" He turned to face me.

"It's yours," I said with a sigh.

"You don't know that," he snapped. "The way you fuck around, it could be anyone's." His voice had turned to venom. I nodded and put the lid back on the marker and returned it to its place on the top box.

"It could be, you're right, but"—I nodded and looked around, still avoiding his stare—"it's yours, I'm sure."

"You're high, fucking high as hell. What do you think you're going to do— trap me into marrying you?" I shook my head. "I've heard of crazy bitches like you, trapping poor fuckers like me with a kid. You're fucking crazy."

I finally met his eyes. He stood on the top step of the porch and towered over me. "You know, I'm not sure if that's a compliment or an insult. If I were to trap someone, it wouldn't be the likes of you."

"I bet you're one of those pro-lifers, aren't you?"

"No," I retorted.

"Well, there you have it. Get an abortion. I'll pay half," he began. I cut him off.

"Pro-choice means I get a choice. You don't get that?" I rolled my eyes. "Choice, pro-*choice*! It's not pro-abortion, you fucking idiot! I'm keeping the baby." The words rang true to my soul. "I don't need you. I just wanted to let you know I'm going to become a mother." I turned and walked back to my car.

A month later, as I was leaving for work, a large bouquet of flowers was delivered with my name on them. The card read, *It's not too late*, *Scott*. Below that were the phone number and address for the local Planned Parenthood.

The only other conversation I had with Scott during my entire pregnancy occurred when he called asking about the sex of the baby. "If it's a boy, a boy needs his daddy. If it's a girl, well ..." he said, followed by a long pause. "I already have a daughter with someone else. I don't need another girl."

A pounding of red blasted my temples and behind my eyes. The hair on the back of my neck stood up. "You shallow piece of shit," I heard myself say. "You'll not find out until it's born."

"Don't be like that—" Enraged, I hung up without letting him finish.

Because of that conversation, I started doing research about what it would take to have him relinquish all parental rights. It also convinced me that no one needed to know the sex of the baby before it was born, not even me.

Taking the card off the flower arrangement, I ripped it up and flushed it down the toilet. I found a notepad and wrote a note to Suzy: *Thank you for putting up with me. I've got good news and bad news. Let's do lunch. Love you.* Then I set the flowers in the middle of the kitchen table with the card I'd written for Suzy. I couldn't hide my pregnancy with baggy clothes much longer, and she deserved to know I was having a baby. She also needed to know that I was planning to move out when the baby arrived.

When I told Suzy, she was ecstatic, but I hesitated before adding I'd be moving out when the baby came. She smiled and said, "Of course you are," and then she volunteered to throw me a baby shower.

Thankfully, my coworkers were just as supportive about the pregnancy.

My belly grew, and summer turned to fall. The doctor had estimated that the baby's due date was October 12. Ironically, that was also the sperm donor's birthday. I rubbed my swollen stomach and pleaded with my unborn child, *You can do better than sharing your birthday with that jerk.*

On the morning of October 10, I was positive I was in labor. I called in to work, started my maternity leave, and grabbed my overnight bag. Suzy drove me to the hospital. Once we got there, the nurses examined me, confirming that I was in the early stages of labor. I was actually excited. But then they informed me that since I hadn't dilated any and my water hadn't broken yet, they'd have to send me home. Suzy held my hand as we walked back to the car.

"Let's go to lunch," she suggested.

At two o'clock on the morning of the eleventh, I woke Suzy up and told her something was wrong. I was in so much pain I thought I was dying, but she stayed calm. "I doubt anything is wrong," she said. "Labor is a bitch. I mean, it really hurts. Bad."

We arrived at the emergency entrance, and the nurse on duty examined me but said I hadn't dilated enough for them to admit me. At this, a primal urge flared within me.

"I'm not going anywhere!" I roared, spittle flying from my lips. Suzy placed her hand on my arm, her eyes pleading with the nurse to save her from the monster I was becoming.

"Well, since your water hasn't broken, you can go relax in the hot tub," the nurse offered. "Perhaps that will help you relax enough to start dilating."

At this suggestion, my blood pressure returned to normal, and I took several deep breaths, bracing myself for the oncoming contraction.

The warm water worked. Once I started to dilate, the whole labor went fast. After two hard pushes, I screamed and faded into my pain. When I arched my back and opened my eyes, my mom's face appeared on the ceiling. *You're doing fine,* she said.

When they placed my baby girl in my hands, she stopped crying. Suzy cut the umbilical cord, tears streaming down her tanned face. My perfect daughter slipped all but one finger into her mouth. We laughed as she stretched her middle finger up and out and gave us all the bird.

She's got your spunk, my mom said.

Suzy headed home to get some sleep, and I settled into the idea of motherhood. The phone beside me rang and jolted me out of my daydream. "Hello?"

"Hey, it's Scott."

My mouth went dry. "What do you want?"

"I had a dream you had the baby." There were several moments of silence. "I've called every hospital in the valley trying to find you. In my dream, it was a girl. Was I right?" More silence. "I'm coming down there."

"Wait!" I spoke up before he disconnected the call. "Does this mean you're going to be a dad? Step up to the plate, be around for your offspring? I didn't think you wanted another daughter." My voice dripped with sarcasm.

The silence went on for so long I thought he'd hung up. "Um … about that," he said and sighed. "I don't want to be a dad; I just wanted to see her. See you."

"Trying to trap me in a relationship?" I asked coolly.

"No, no, it's not that. I just … I don't know, Dacia. I thought I'd make an effort."

"Today or for the next twenty years?" More silence. "Listen"—my voice was sharp and bitter—"I've got one sweet deal for you. Are you listening to me?"

"I'm listening."

"I won't put your name on the birth certificate, I won't sue you for child support, but here's my one and only condition." There was a beat of time between us, the tension building. I took a deep breath. "You never lay eyes on her. You never darken our door. You never call me or talk to me, or her, again. You got it?"

"I knew it was a girl. What'd you name her?"

"If you don't comply with my one and only request, I'll garnish wages from you for the next twenty years. Do you hear me?"

"What'd you name her?" he asked again.

From nowhere, I said, "Devin."

"Aw, that's a nice name. Could have been good for a boy or girl. I like it." Another long silence ensued between us. "Your offer sounds too good to be true. What's the hitch, Dee?"

"There's no hitch. It's all or nothing. You're her dad, or you're not. It's that simple. Some things aren't about *you.*"

"Okay, I get it. I'm out."

"Just so we're on the same page …" I composed my thoughts and looked at the baby sleeping soundlessly in the bassinet beside me. Her cheeks were flushed, her tiny hand balled into a miniature fist. "If you have a 'Golly gee, I should be a dad to my daughter' moment in the future, I'm telling you right now, I'll make it hard on you. Not only will you have to find us, but you'll have to pay for a paternity test and be current on all child support arrears; otherwise, the answer to seeing her is no."

"I'll leave you both alone. I expect you to be a woman of *your* word."

"You don't have to worry about that," I said without emotion.

"Okay."

"Okay."

"Have a good life, Dacia."

"Sure will, Scott." I hung up and reached for little Devin. She nuzzled my chest and curled into me. Life started now.

CHAPTER 39

The next morning, after the maternity ward nurse left, Suzy was the first person to come visit us.

"Hey," she cooed, "let's see that pretty girl." She took Devin from me. "We should probably talk."

"Yeah? What about?"

She looked at Devin but talked to me. "What's going to happen next?"

"What do you mean?" I was confused.

"Are you planning on staying?"

"At your house? Yes. Where else would I go?"

She shrugged. "I don't know. I just want to make sure you're going to stay off that shit, you know. For Devi's sake, my kids' sake, your sake. For everyone, you know?" I nodded and felt tears rush to my eyes. I was so lucky to be here, blessed beyond belief that I had a friend like Suzy who wanted the best for me even though I hadn't been the best friend to her. Bigger than the moment was I had a reliable job, complete with insurance benefits, so I could support my new infant.

"Thank you," I managed to say.

"Knock, knock." Joy's voice rang out as the door opened. "Good morning, mama," she sang.

"I've got to run," Suzy said and handed me Devin. I peered down at her sleeping face and wondered, again, how I had created such a perfect baby. "When the doctors say you can go, just call me. I'll come get you."

"Thanks," I said to her back as she left. I put Devin back in the bassinet next to my bed.

Joy brought two wrapped boxes; in one box was a white bunting with one blue pompom and one pink pompom clustered on one side of the front. An embroidered rabbit decorated the opposite side. "So the baby has something nice to come home in. Wasn't sure of the sex, so I got a gift that could go either way," she explained.

I smiled and reached for the second gift. It was a box of oracle cards—angel cards, to be specific. "Sometimes your angels have no other way to communicate other than through these cards." She took them from the box and handed them to me. "Pick three. I'll show you."

I shuffled them, cut the deck in the center, pulled the top three cards, and laid them facedown. I flipped the first one. It was the Healthy Lifestyle card. She smiled.

"The positions of the cards are as important as the cards themselves. The first card drawn is what brought you to your current situation. Ironic, don't you think?"

I smiled and flipped the next card. It was Self-Acceptance, and it was upside down.

"When cards come upside down like that, it's an area of resistance or difficulty. The second card is the obstacle, the challenge." Tears filled my eyes. "Love yourself," she said, touching my hand. "The last card is the outcome card." I turned it faceup—New Beginnings. "I don't think I have to explain that one." Her smile was warm and comforting.

There was a knock on the door. "Expecting someone?" Joy moved to open the door, but it swung before she reached it.

"Oh, I'm sorry. Am I interrupting?" It was Dean Martin, the nurse from rehab. Joy looked him over, mumbling some excuse to leave. She turned and winked at me as the door closed behind her.

"I was in the neighborhood. Thought I'd drop by and see how you're doing!" I was speechless. He looked down at Devin wrapped in her blanket. "I'm so glad you got your shit together, Dacia." He reached out and let his finger graze Devin's back. "One of our patients was arrested. She was high and pregnant, went into labor, and the baby was born extremely premature." He turned so our eyes met. "Her son is only two pounds. I'm worried he isn't going to make it."

"That's so sad," I said as reality hit me—that could have been little Devin.

"Yeah, that's why I'm really here—to check on them. Getting to see you is just a bonus." His dark blue eyes sparkled when he smiled. He sat on the edge of my bed and picked up my hand. "How have you been?"

"I've had my ups and downs, but I'm ready for a new chapter." I looked down at his hand and noticed a tan line where his wedding ring should have been. He saw me looking.

"My wife left me."

"Oh, that's too bad," I answered, letting my hand linger just a moment too long.

"Not really. We didn't get along very well. We were together because of our daughter, Ryver. That's it. We had nothing else in common. Not sure we were ever really in love, to be honest."

"Wow." I had no idea what else to say. I picked up my daughter and focused on her for a moment as he continued.

"I've thought about you over the months, wondered about you, you know." I nodded slowly, encouraging him to continue. "I am here about that little guy I was telling you about, but—" I lowered my eyes to the sleeping baby. "What are these?" he asked, picking up the cards Joy had left.

"Apparently, they're your angel's way of telling you what to do," I said, smiling.

"Like the tarot?"

"Yeah, but nicer," I said as he cut the deck. "Just draw out any three cards."

He shuffled and cut the deck and then flipped the first card. It was the Romance card, upside down. The next card he flipped over was also upside down, representing Children, and the last card, New Love.

"Well, what do you make of that?" He laughed as he stared at the three cards lined out between us.

"I don't know. I just got them today," I answered and leaned in and kissed him.

"Whoa! What are you doing?" he said, obviously surprised as he jerked his head away from me.

"I, um—" I was floundering for words.

"Listen, Dacia, just because I was thinking about you and wondered how you are getting on doesn't mean I want to sleep with you." My embarrassment burned the back of my neck and exploded onto my cheeks. I looked at the baby in my arms to hide the awkwardness.

"I mean"—he dragged his hand over his face and stood a bit straighter—"it's not like I don't want to have sex with you. It's just that, well ..." Our eyes met, and I realized his face was as red as mine. "It's just you've got your hands full, literally and figuratively." I looked back at Devin asleep in my arms. "And besides, I'm on the rebound." I nodded and felt tears of shame well up in my eyes.

"Catch you on the flip side, pretty girl," he said gently and bent over, kissing the top of my head. With that, he disappeared into the hospital, the door closing with a hard thump.

"Looks like it's just me and you, kiddo," I whispered to the sleeping babe as the tears continued to streak down my face. Her tiny bow lips curled into a closed-mouth grin when she heard my voice, her eyes remained closed, and she looked like the most content, perfect baby in the world. The deck of angel cards seemed to glow and call out to me. I reached over and cut the deck. It was the Truth and Integrity card. I flipped open the little guidebook and read, "Let go of anything inauthentic and all activities that do not mirror your highest intentions for yourself."

You've got this, I heard come from somewhere deep within my chest, and I knew, without a doubt, I did.

ABOUT THE AUTHOR

D. W. Plato has been known to say, "Give me thirty minutes in a hostel, hotel, or hospital, and I can walk out with a novel idea." With her ability to easily make friends combined with her gift of gab and an overactive imagination, this statement isn't a stretch.

She's been writing for as long as she can remember and has always dreamed of being published. With the ease with which self-publishing is available in today's world because of modern technology, she thought, *Why not go for it?*

Check out her premier novel, *The Sinners' Club*, as well as D. W.'s first historical fiction novel, *Trials and Tribulations of Modesty Greene*, about Harriet Tubman's historical legacy.

Printed in the United States
By Bookmasters